BROTHERS AT WAR

Don Cummer

Scholastic Canada Ltd.
Toronto New York London Auckland Sydney
Mexico City New Delhi Hong Kong Buenos Aires

Scholastic Canada Ltd.
604 King Street West, Toronto, Ontario M5V 1E1, Canada

Scholastic Inc.
557 Broadway, New York, NY 10012, USA

Scholastic Australia Pty Limited
PO Box 579, Gosford, NSW 2250, Australia

Scholastic New Zealand Limited
Private Bag 94407, Botany, Manukau 2163, New Zealand

Scholastic Children's Books
Euston House, 24 Eversholt Street, London NW1 1DB, UK

www.scholastic.ca

Library and Archives Canada Cataloguing in Publication
Cummer, Don, 1952-, author
Brothers at war / Don Cummer.

Issued in print and electronic formats.
ISBN 978-1-4431-1382-3 (pbk.).–ISBN 978-1-4431-2848-3 (html)

1. Canada–History–War of 1812–Juvenile fiction. I. Title.

PS8605.U44B76 2013   jC813'.6   C2013-901788-7
C2013-901789-5

6 5 4 3 2 1   Printed in Canada 121   13 14 15 16 17

MIX
Paper from
responsible sources
FSC   **FSC® C004071**
www.fsc.org

TABLE OF CONTENTS

For William Jackson Cummer
(1922–2013)

Dare and Consequences

February 1811

I have been chosen first. Me. Jacob Gibson. Hero-in-waiting.

Shoulders back like a soldier. Snowballs in my mitts. My faithful attack dog at my side. (Well, Ginger is actually romping about with the new boy.) And beneath my coat and shirt, my magic medicine bag to protect me.

First. Bravest. Best.

I wasn't exactly first. The older boys were picked before me — both the towners and the dockers.

Then William Dunwoody said, "We'll take Gibson."

But of all the young boys, I am first. The older boys know me by name. No one knows the name of the new boy.

He moved here last week and lives at the foot of King Street, where his father bought the tannery. He smells like a tannery too. He's probably a docker rather than a towner, but none of the sons of the fishermen and longshoremen welcome him.

William didn't even bother to learn his name. After even the youngest boys had been picked, he said, "I suppose that means we have to take this one."

And the new boy just grinned.

On the other side of the field, waits the enemy. They've built a big snow fort, but stand before its walls, ready for our attack.

Farther up the hill, a pair of sentries watches from the bastion of Fort George — real soldiers and a real fort. They hold their muskets in the crooks of their arms and tuck their hands up the sleeves of their greatcoats.

And in between, from the wooden palisade to the frozen river, a carpet of fresh snow. Soft, moist snow. Snowball snow.

Only two sets of tracks spoil that pure white field. One shows where Ginger trotted toward the enemy and squatted to do her business. And then, following her tracks, *his* boot prints. They stop where he stooped to pick up the steaming turds and put them in a small canvas bag. At the tannery, they use dog droppings along with human piss to make the leather soft. The boys on the other side of the field hooted and laughed.

He's drawn attention to himself. When the snowballs fly, he will be a target — that's for sure. Best not to stand too close.

I stare forward. But Ginger has other ideas. She prances around the new boy and jumps up with her paws on his chest. He has picked up her mess. In the dog world, that must count for something. "Ginger! Down!" I command.

But she bounces and yaps, and licks the new boy's face, then twirls and lies on her back for a belly rub. The new boy grins at me and, in spite of myself, I like him: his toothy smile, a mop of black hair, and bright blue eyes. He's small and skinny, like me.

"Mister Gibson," a voice snaps. "Can you control that dog of yours?"

"Yes, sir."

William Dunwoody has called me "Mister." Any boy would feel lucky if he said hello — let alone called him *Mister*. And he has chosen *me*. *First!*

"I want you in reserve, Gibson."

Reserve? In a snowball fight?

"You and Turd Boy here."

Turd Boy? The other boys snicker. Poor fellow — he'll never live this down. Might as well pack his bags and head west to the Indian country.

The new boy stands, head high. "Sure, Junior," he replies calmly. "Whatever you like . . . Junior."

He pronounces "like" as *lahk* — drawn out and relaxed — an accent that comes from way beyond the other side of the river. But never mind that. *Junior?* Doesn't the new boy know who he is talking to?

Junior . . . Obviously he does! I suck in my breath and glance at the others. Trouble ahead. William's father is also named William Dunwoody — the richest man in town with his ships, his warehouses and his contracts to feed the army. He's also the magistrate for Lincoln County. His son likes to call himself William Dunwoody II. "Junior" might stick worse than "Turd Boy."

They stare at each other. Even on a winter day, William leaves his overcoat open and his cravat untied. Only William would wear a cravat to a snowball fight. He stands tall, with his feet firm, and he turns his head to glance at me, then back down at the new boy. His green eyes narrow. Hungry eyes — he eats his revenge cold.

"Gibson," he says, "never mind the reserve. You and this one will lead the attack. You're the Forlorn Hope."

In Newark, we see soldiers every day and learn early what they do, and how they do it. The Forlorn Hope is the detail that leads the attack on a fort. It's a deadly job. Those few soldiers face cannons, muskets and hand bombs. They rarely come back alive, but if they do, they are heroes.

That's the new boy and me, crossing the slope, heroes. I march straight ahead. Chin high. No ducking or flinching. In my mind, the flags snap, the fifes toodle and the drums rat-a-tat-tat.

Some talk of Alexander, and some of Hercules,
Of Hector and Lysander and such great names
as these . . .

On the bastion of Fort George, more soldiers have joined the sentries to watch us. I'll show them how Upper Canada boys march into battle. Eyes front!

But I glance to my left. The new boy isn't stepping straight into the face of death like a soldier. He stalks like an Indian, crouching head down as he runs, waits, then runs again.

That's how Father fought long ago when the colonies rebelled. We are civilized now. I will fight like a real soldier. Hard to do, with Ginger leaping up and tugging at my sleeve.

My leather pouch hangs on a strap around my neck. Is its medicine powerful enough to turn aside a snowball — a volley of snowballs? The magic of Father's Mohawk friend, Tako'skó:wa, Mountain Lion. My magic now.

But of all the world's great heroes,
There's none that can compare . . .

The enemy waits. Most boys carry a snowball in one hand and an armload of snowballs in the other. But Henry Ecker stands with just one snowball in each hand. He towers over the other boys and higher than the walls of their fort.

The new boy pays Henry no mind. He skirts to the left, as sneaky as a weasel . . . no, with that big grin on his face, as playful as an otter!

With a tow row row and a tow row row
To the British grenadiers.

Henry cocks his arm. His followers prepare to throw. Here it comes. I lift my head and stare straight at Henry.

And that's when the snowball hits him. Right in the face. He loses his feet and trips over two smaller boys and all three of them tumble into the snow. Across the slope, the new boy is as surprised as I am. Then a snowball smashes into the back of my head, and I spin around and catch a blizzard. But not from the boys on the other side. From Fort George!

There on the bastion, the men of His Majesty's 41st Regiment of Foot laugh and cheer as they pelt us. I doubt they've had this much fun since they were boys themselves in England. A lesson: never start a snowball fight within range of real soldiers and a real fort.

There is only one thing to do. I turn and face the fire from the bastion.

"Charge!"

* * *

On the top of the slope, Fort George lies so low to the ground that you can see rooftops over the palisades. On the corner bastions, cannons point across the river at the United States. I sprint toward those guns.

I throw as hard as I can, but my snowball lands in the ditch below the earthworks. Closer! Closer! Charge!

Henry Ecker and his crew scramble up the slope to my left, and William Dunwoody and his boys to the right — all one team now. Ginger scampers after one snowball and buries her nose into the powder where it lands. Then she whips around to chase after another. I press ahead. My second snowball splatters on a gun and sprays a soldier in the face. He laughs.

The bastions of Fort George are protected by a dry ditch. At the edge, I cock my hand to fire. A snowball smashes my wrist and it stings like a strapping. I double over and whip off my woollen mitts — they're soaking wet and so I fling them to the ground. My hands are colder but my aim is better. My next snowball hits a soldier in the neck. On the lip of the ditch, I kneel to pack another shot.

"No, Ginger! Get down!"

My balance shifts. No ground beneath. Nothing but the steep slope and the drifts, far below. I tumble down the ditch and flounder at the bottom in a spray of snow.

Above me, a hailstorm of snowballs hurls back and forth across the sky. Ginger can scamper up and down the sides, but when I try to climb, I slip.

At the top, William strikes a heroic pose. Snowballs whip past but nothing can touch him.

"William! Help me!"

He packs a snowball and throws.

"Captain! Down here! Get me out!"

I stretch out my hand. He looks down at me, puzzled — trying to recollect who I am.

"Help!" I shout.

A snowball smashes into his cheek and he snarls words that I would get my mouth washed with soap for repeating. He backs away from the lip of the ditch and I can't see him. The voices of the other boys fade. They're in retreat. I'm trapped.

But the new boy plummets over the lip of the ditch and tumbles like an avalanche. He slams me back to where the soldiers cannot see us, then sits against the logs.

"I'm Eli." *Aam Ee-lah.* He holds out his mittened hand. "Eli McCabe."

"Jacob Gibson."

"I know." *Ah know.* "Your pa has that there store on Pree-dew Street."

He butchers that name. I take his hand but he stops in mid-shake and stares. My hands look as cold and raw as they feel.

"Where's your mitts?"

I nod toward the top of the ditch and he clucks in sympathy. "Here. Take mine. I reckon I don't need 'em so bad."

He reaches into his coat and pulls out a pocket

knife. He removes one mitt but it hangs suspended from his cuff. It's fastened by a woollen string which he cuts with a flick of his knife. I curl my fists into balls inside his mitts and bury them beneath my armpits.

"What's that?" Eli asks.

My medicine bundle has slipped out from my shirt — a buckskin bag, the size of a child's fist. I try to tuck it back under my shirt, but the mitts are clumsy and my fingers slow.

"A gift," I snap. He shrugs. I add more kindly, "From a friend of my father."

He looks at me with new curiosity. "Looks Injun. Your pa friends with Injuns?"

I stare off up the slope and he does not press the question.

Ginger returns from the front lines, panting happily. She settles between us and I slip off a mitt and bury my hand in the warmth beneath her fur. The battle hurls over us.

"You reckon this thing is just about over?"

I think a moment. "They'll run out of snow. On the ramparts."

He nods. "That's pretty smart, Jake. Real tackle-kill."

"Tactical?"

"That's right. Reckon we can wait it out here."

And we do. The battle ends and we rise to our

feet. The sun is burning through the clouds and the snow sparkles bright on the slope above us. "How we gonna get out?" he asks.

"Go around to the gate, I suppose."

"Aw, that ain't no fun. Here. Climb on me."

He stands at the foot of the ditch and leans back as stiff as a pine tree.

"Timberrrrr!" He laughs as he falls. "Come on, I ain't gonna wait all day," he says as he clasps his hands to lift my foot.

I get ready to climb up, but he changes his mind. Now he flaps his arms up and down in the snow. He makes angel wings. When he's finished, he boosts me up over his head. From the top I reach down for him.

Down the hillside, the other boys have gathered by the river at the Navy Hall. When they see us coming, they part before us and close up again. We're the heroes who led the charge, and now we will be knighted by the leaders. That's what I think.

With their backs to the storehouse, William and Henry sit on barrels, like kings on their thrones. William is tall and elegant, but even he looks small beside Henry.

"Here's Turd Boy now," William sneers. "We've got a score to settle."

Henry slides off the barrel and steps toward Eli. "This one?"

William slips onto the ground with the ease of a

cat. "Plucky," he says, "but he doesn't know his place." The other boys back away. Will the dock boys stand up for Eli? But no one steps forward.

"So," says William, "you want to join our games? First you have to pass a test."

"He's already passed the test," I blurt. "He came to my help."

"That was *your* test, Gibson," sneers William. "Now let's see what Turd Boy is really made of." He stares across the ice that stretches to the American side of the river. A quarter mile down, where the ice widens into the lake, Fort Niagara towers on the American shore like some castle from another time, another place.

William says loudly enough for all to hear, "You want to run with us, Turd Boy?"

I suck in my breath. This doesn't sound good.

Henry points across to the far shore. "The Yankee side of the river, Turd Boy. Let's see you run there and back. In . . . let's make it ten minutes."

No one says a word. In the depth of winter, the river freezes over from shoreline to shoreline, but nobody trusts it. The water is swift and the eddies strong. The boulders of ice are treacherous and the layer of snow hides the current that swirls just below the surface.

Finally I speak up. "Are you daft?"

"You scared, Gibson?" Henry asks.

"I'll bet Turd Boy here isn't," William adds. He doesn't take his eyes from Eli. If he were a cat, his tail would swish as he waited to pounce.

Eli's eyes question mine. He turns to Henry. "I dunno, Lug. I reckon my pa'd thrash me."

Henry bristles. "Then stay with your daddy. And your mommy too."

William cuts in. "Won't cross the river? Then how about this side? That your house?" He points down-river beyond the marsh. "You run there and back. Ten minutes."

And then Henry adds, "You're chicken-hearted, Turd Boy. *Buck-buck-buuuuuck.*"

How dare they pick on him. He's the only one who had enough courage to rescue me. The rest of them ran cowering.

If they think they can single the new boy out like this, they've got another think coming.

I step forward onto the ice, before anyone can say anything else.

I'll show them who's scared and who's not.

Ginger's not scared either. She whimpers and whines, then barks. But she would never leave me to face danger alone. She passes me, pressing her muzzle to the ground. I follow her footprints.

Ten yards. Twenty. Fifty. I follow Ginger's tracks and listen carefully. No sound of water. Birds in the cattails to my left. Harness bells farther off in the distance.

Behind me, a boot crunches on snow. Eli following? I don't look back.

With her nose down and ears up, Ginger takes a roundabout route, weaving toward the far bank, then back toward our side. She stops to watch me. Then she heads toward the shoreline.

Not yet! We're so close to the tannery now. Her route makes no sense to me and I step off her trail.

In Newark, we grow up knowing ice and snow and the telltale sounds when the river will not hold. First the sharp crack, like someone has snapped a stick. Then smaller snaps, like crunching a pine cone. And if you don't move back to safety, one big crack as loud as a bullwhip, followed by the splash.

But that's not what happens. Just a short, sharp *thud* before the splash. My feet plunge into the water.

Somewhere beneath that surface of sparkling snow, the river has made this trap, and I've sprung it. The cold stabs into my breastbone and strangles my throat. I cannot breathe. But the hole is small. A chunk of ice sticks up like a frozen spire. I grab it and hold on with all my strength.

A tug-tug-tug on my shoulder, pulling me against the current. Ginger. Teeth clenched on my coat.

Someone's hand. Someone stretching on the ice, reaching out. Eli. What's he doing here? It's dangerous. Doesn't he know that? I cannot take my eyes away from his. Blue eyes that drill into mine. He's shouting at me, but I hear only the rushing water.

Time slows. My body swings away from me, fluttering beneath the ice like a banner. The current is more powerful than horses, as unstoppable as a blizzard. It roars down from the giant lakes upstream, and nothing can prevent it reaching the sea. It will drag all three of us under.

My hands can't feel Eli's hands now. But he does not let go. His eyes squint and his teeth are set like he's biting something really hard. My eyelashes freeze. Water slaps my face, roars past my ears. Another hand on my arm now. Two hands. *Big* hands. I rise. And the air hits my wet clothes and it feels even colder than the water.

I am lifted by powerful arms. I am wrapped in a grey overcoat and heaved over someone's shoulder. There are epaulettes on that shoulder. Epaulettes of bright gold. I can't keep my eyes open. So sleepy.

I drift up to the surface of a dream and break free into the air. Weight of a buffalo robe. My teeth chatter and my body shakes. Someone opens my mouth and a liquid burns. I sputter and cough.

I'm lying on the seat of a sleigh, and I whisk through the town. The runners hiss over the snow. I recognize a tree, a rooftop. Mother's face looks down. Why so frightened?

Lifted again. Father. And a big man, the one with epaulettes. Like a general's. I focus my eyes on the gold braiding and how they dangle from his shoulders.

Mother's face close to mine. Here's Cathleen, our hired woman. She holds the door open. She crosses herself. Warm smells. Wood smoke. Barley soup. Bacon. Home.

Wet clothes peeled away. Father on his knees, rubbing my feet. The kitchen fire. Cathleen stoking up the logs.

Mother presses my cheeks and I open my lips. Warm tea hot on my tongue. I swallow and a glow spreads through me like a stain.

I want to dive back down into that dream. My eyes are so heavy. The fire rises in the hearth. On the stone ledge, my medicine bundle lies like a drowned mouse. My eyelids sink heavier, and I float up with the mist.

And as I drift away, I think of the bright blue eyes of Eli McCabe. This morning, we didn't even know each other.

HOME

February 1811

"Father?"

His face snaps up. He places a ribbon on the page and closes the book. His eyes drink in mine and the smile spreads across his face.

"Yes, Jacob."

"How long have I been asleep?"

He reaches across the blankets and takes my hand.

"Two days." Still he does not rise from the chair. His fingers are strong and his palms hard and calloused. He calls out without taking his eyes from mine, "Jane?" And again, louder, "Jane!"

My lungs feel as though they're full of water. I begin to cough, and I keep coughing. I can't stop. Father takes a towel that lies beside my bed and wipes my mouth. I gasp for breath and ask, "Where's Ginger?"

"The kitchen."

From down the stairs, she yips joyfully.

"Can she come upstairs? Just this once?"

He shakes his head. "When you're better, you'll go down to see her."

He calls out again, "Jane?"

"There were epaulettes . . . "

He nods. I sit up against the headboard.

"General Brock."

He squeezes my hands and begins to chuckle. I close my mouth and swallow hard. General Brock, the most important man in all of Upper Canada . . .

"*Him?*"

"Yes. He went out on the ice."

Then from downstairs, "Robert?" I try to rise, but the room swims around my head. Mother's footsteps climb the stairs — so much heavier these days. "Robert?" she calls again, "Is he . . . ?"

The door swings open and her face glows, even through the tears. Beside me on the bed, her shoulders shake as she sobs into my hair. I hold her so tight I can feel her heart beat.

"My Jacob . . . "

"I'm all right, Mama."

* * *

Next morning, I'm strong enough to rise to my window. I melt the ice with my palm. By the water well, Ginger lies in her doghouse with her nose on her paws. She looks up at me and scampers to her feet, tail wagging. If I had a tail, it would wag too.

Up Prideaux Street comes Father with Dr. Kerr. I scurry back to bed and my heart races as their footsteps climb the stairs. The doctor puts his bag down and glances at the window where my peephole is starting to freeze in the shape of my palm.

"You nearly caught your death, young man. Another minute and it would have been over for you. We'll see whether that inflammation turns into pneumonia. So! You'll stay in bed 'til you're good and rested, laddie. Lots of sleep. Tea. Cod liver oil. And I suppose you can start having visitors."

Good! I want to see my new best friend.

But my first visitor is not Eli. I recognize the *thud* of a walking stick. The door bursts open.

"Young Master Gibson, am I welcome here? You've been in a spot of mischief. Eh?"

Father's friend, Mr. Willcocks, fills the doorway. He twirls his walking stick and lays it on the chair together with his top hat. He steps forward and reaches out his hand, then clasps mine in both his big paws. "You'll be aright, young fellow," he grins, "right as roosters." He pumps my hand. "And we'll write you up in my newspaper, lad," he continues. "You and that fine Ginger of yours." His hand draws across the air, picturing the headline. "*Brave dog rescues boy from river.*"

"But what about Eli?"

"The tanner's boy? Oh, yes. The young hero too."

"And what about General Brock?"

Mr. Willcocks's laugh has a merry Irish lilt. "Oh, the General's got enough admirers in this colony as 'tis, wouldn't you say? No, my lad, it's you two and Ginger we'll make famous."

That evening I shuffle down to the kitchen. Ginger licks my face and hands, and rolls on her back. She wants to play, but I just sit by the fire and scratch her behind the ears. Mother helps me back to my room, supporting me with one arm while she carries the candle in her other hand. It is I who ought to be helping her. I'm almost as tall as she is. Her belly is so big it's really obvious now that she's expecting a baby.

"Mother?"

"Yes, Jacob."

"Will you stay and read to me tonight?"

"Let me fetch another candle."

I listen to her footsteps retreat down to the lobby — she needs all her strength to make those stairs. I lie back, staring at the candle flame. Then I hear the knock on the front door.

William Dunwoody's voice carries clearly up the stairs. "Mrs. Gibson, how well you look." He sounds so bright and cheery, but it sends a chill down my spine.

Henry's voice adds, "We've come to inquire about poor Jacob."

Mother's reply is lost as they move to the parlour. She should keep them in the lobby — welcome them in the front door, hustle them out the back door. That would put them in their place!

Mother instructs Cathleen to prepare tea as Father comes in from the stable. Chairs scrape as William and Henry rise to greet him.

"We've brought gifts, Mrs. Gibson. My mother sends you this honey with her best wishes." Mother's response is too soft for me to hear. "And this," William continues, "is for Jacob."

Whatever it is, I don't want it.

"I'll see if he can come down," she says.

"I'll do that," says Father.

"No. He's waiting for me," she replies.

Mother's footsteps heave their way up the stairs. I blow out the candle, snuggle down under the blankets and pretend to sleep. She stands in the doorway a long moment before returning to the parlour.

On tiptoe I creep out to the landing at the top of the stairs above the lobby. I often do this when Mother and Father are up late with dinner guests — eavesdrop from the railing while they think I'm asleep. But I've never listened so hard as tonight.

"We tried to stop him," says William. "I have no idea what possessed him to go out onto the ice."

Father's voice is guarded. "We're fortunate that the McCabe boy was there. And General Brock."

Henry's voice lowers to a rumble and all I can catch is, " . . . every inch a hero."

"The McCabe boy too," adds Mother.

"Oh," agrees William brightly, "of course."

The kitchen door opens on the other side of the lobby, and Cathleen backs through with the tea tray. She glances up. She knows I like to listen like this. Sometimes after a big dinner party, she will bring me tea, but tonight I shake my head.

When it's time for them to go, I slip back into the bedroom and promise myself I will never be on their side in a snowball fight again. Not ever.

* * *

What a ruckus outside. Ginger's yelps and barks bring me to the window to see her wrestling in the snow with Eli. At the front door, his voice is so quiet I cannot hear. "I am pleased to meet you," says Mother. "Jacob's been looking forward to your visit."

His steps skip the stairs two at a time and he stands in the doorway in his best Sunday clothes and his hair carefully combed. That's not the boy I remember, but his big smile and bright blue eyes are the same. He carries Mr. Willcocks's newspaper, the *Upper Canada Guardian*, and a box wrapped in ribbon.

"Ma made 'em for you." He thrusts the box toward me and drops the newspaper on the chair. I smell oatmeal cookies even before I untie the ribbon. He sits beside me on the bed and we munch happily. He looks over at the cravat that lies at the foot of my bed.

"What's that?"

"A gift. From Junior. He left it here yesterday."

Eli picks it up and runs the length of fine linen across his fingers.

"Nice. You gonna wear it?"

I shake my head.

"Might be some use for it." He loops it around and draws the end down again.

"Tug-o'-war," I reply. "With Ginger."

"Naw . . . " Eli wraps the end of the cravat around the loop he has made. One, two, three, four . . . "We can find better things than that." Five, six, seven . . . "Nope, not long enough after all." He holds up his handiwork for me to admire. "There's s'posed to be thirteen." He has knotted a hangman's noose out of William's gift.

I laugh. "Send Junior to the gallows with a linen rope. He'd like that."

"Him? He'd want silk. Before I forget . . . " He picks up the newspaper from the chair and thrusts it at me. "You and me's in it. I heard say."

I grasp the paper. "Where? Are we famous?"

"I reckon. Dunno. Can't read."

I look up to see if he's joking.

He grins. "So you read to me, Jake."

I'm a good reader — the best in the classroom. But I don't have the trick of reading a newspaper quickly the way Father does. I need to read the first sentences of each story before I know what it's about.

The column begins by saying that some people in the United States Congress want to go to war with Britain. Farther down the page, the apothecary has camphor gum, juniper oil, orange peel, rhubarb and female pills.

"What's female pills?" Eli asks.

"Maybe they're pills to make you into a girl."

Eli shudders in disgust, then adds, "I'll ask my sister. She'll know."

The next columns have longer stories. Napoleon's armies are trying to capture a city in Spain. Nothing about us, so I move on.

And then, there it is!

I read to Eli: *Boy Rescued from River.* And underneath it a second headline: *Faithful dog and immigrant son heroes of the day.*

Eli whoops and hops onto his hands and knees beside me. I read:

A canine companion and the son of the local tanner were the heroes when, with the help of the local military, they pulled a Newark boy from the icy waters of the Niagara River. Jacob Gibson, son of the respected Prideaux Street merchant, had suffered the misadventure and would have perished were it not for the fast thinking and courage of Eli McCabe and the Gibson dog. The boy continues to recover satisfactorily.

I stop reading. Eli waits.

"That's all," I say. "What do you have to do to have a big story? Conquer Spain?" Poor Ginger didn't even have her name in the story at all. And then it occurs to me. Neither did General Brock.

But Eli leans over with shining eyes. "Show me my name!"

* * *

After that, Eli comes by every morning, and Mother begins to teach him his ABCs, just like she did with me when I was little. We can make a towner of him yet.

We sit by the fire in the kitchen and Cathleen brings us tea with milk and lots of sugar. Ginger lies between us with her nose toward the coals.

"Father thinks I'm almost well enough to go thank General Brock. He says you can come too."

I thought that Eli would be excited, but he frowns.

"Eli, what's wrong?"

"Don't know if I should see the General."

"Why not?"

"Might get Pa in trouble."

"What on earth for?"

"He ain't swore yet."

"What?"

"He ain't swore allegiance."

"To the King?"

"That's right. And they say that Junior's pa's gonna

throw us out of the Canadas if he don't swear."

"Who says?"

"Mr. McKenney for one. Can't own property if he ain't swore at the King."

"*To* the King."

"That's right."

"Then why doesn't your father just take the oath?"

"My pa swears at everything — cowhides, piss jugs, nails to be hammered. But he ain't gonna swear at no king in England."

"Anyone from across the river has to swear that oath, Eli."

"So they say."

"He must have known that."

Eli nods. "I reckon he figured there'd be a lot more people up here who felt like he does."

"There's lots of Americans, yes."

"Guess the others ain't so stubborn like my pa."

"Eli, he's come to Upper Canada. He's got to obey King George."

"Only George my pa respects is George Washington. My grandpappy fought for him in the war."

"Father was in the war too."

"He know George Washington?"

"Eli, my father was on the other side."

"A *Tory?*" He raises his voice. "Them was traitors what fought against Liberty."

I feel hot, and it's not because of the fire. "They

weren't traitors, Eli. They were loyal. They were *Loyalists*. You rebels were the traitors."

"I ain't no rebel. And don't you say that about my grandpappy!" Eli rises to his feet and grabs his coat from the peg. "Nor George Washington neither! He's the Father of Our Country."

Ginger rises and retreats to a far corner under the table.

"You, William Dunwoody, Henry Ecker. You're all on the same side," he shouts from the doorway. "You're all Tories and I don't blame my pa for not swearing your oath."

Eli stomps out of the house. Ginger watches from under the table. And I'm confused.

* * *

"Father?" I put down my quill, careful not to smudge the numbers in my book.

"Yes, Jacob." He does not look up from his account book.

"Did you ever swear allegiance?"

His quill continues to scratch. "Long ago."

"When you were in the war?"

"Somewhere back then." His eyes dart from one page to another, comparing numbers.

"Does everyone swear the oath?"

"Yes."

At the far end of the kitchen table, I return to

my column. Ginger lies asleep by the fire. A storm blusters outside and wind and snow rattle against the windowpane.

"What happens if you don't?"

"Don't what?"

"Swear the oath of allegiance. Can you be put in jail?"

"I wouldn't think so."

"Can they throw you out of the province?"

"Probably."

"But what if you've done nothing wrong?"

Finally he looks up. "Jacob, I want to finish before bedtime."

"Yes, sir." I look at the numbers in my columns again, but can't concentrate to add them up.

"Father?"

"Yes, Jacob."

"Did you ever see George Washington?"

This time he does look up, briefly, annoyed. "No." He returns to his accounting.

"Eli thinks he's the father of our country."

Father gives a long, hard look over his spectacles. "The McCabes have immigrated here. He should know King George is the father of *this* country."

I nod and Father returns to his book.

King George has reigned since Father was a little boy. George Washington died long ago. Maybe Eli thinks that he's still alive. If I tell Father that Eli thinks George Washington is a hero, will he let Eli visit anymore?

Father talks about the American Rebellion only when he thinks I am not within earshot, but when I sit on the landing after dinner, I hear the stories. When he was not much older than me, Father fought at the Battle of Oriskany. Neighbours fought neighbours, and some of the neighbours were Rebels and some were Loyalists and some were Iroquois.

Late at night, after the port has been passed around and the pipes lit, Father and a few of his friends will remember ambuscades and being ambushed. Sometimes they even talk about the killing, and it was not just the soldiers of the rebel armies they had killed — not just the cows and the horses. Not just burned houses and fields. Sometimes women and children were killed too.

"Father?"

"Yes, Jacob." His focus has returned to the account book again.

"You and Henry Ecker's father were both rangers. During the war. Right?"

This time, he puts down his quill and looks at me over his spectacles. "That's right," he says slowly, tentatively — as if testing ice on the river.

"Did you know him?"

"A little."

"Was he at Oriskany?"

"Yes."

Outside, the wind grows louder and shakes the door. Winter is staying very long this year. I glance at the windows, and when I look back, Father is still watching me.

"There were two big differences between Mr. Ecker and me," he says. "For one, he served with Captain Butler — Colonel Butler's son. I was under Captain Coldwell."

A dog barks in the distance. Poor dog, to be out on a night like this. Ginger raises her head, then lowers it to her paws once more. She sighs, cocks an ear and looks at Father. He is listening to the barking too. Or at least, I think he is. His mind has gone off to a different place, like it does sometimes.

Colonel Butler led his rangers from here in Newark. They were Loyalists who used to live along the Mohawk Valley. They wore the green uniforms that some of the old men still put on every June 4 when we celebrate the King's birthday. Father no longer has his. I once asked him where it was. He said he had burned it.

"We've done enough tonight," Father says. "Your mother will be fast asleep."

I cap the inkwell and blot the page. He puts his arm around my shoulder and leads me through the doorway into the lobby. Ginger rises and follows and takes her place at the bottom of the stairs.

"What was the other?" I whisper.

"I beg your pardon?"

"You said there were two differences. Between you and Mr. Ecker."

"Yes . . ."

He guides me up the stairs. We step over the third stair that squeaks so loudly.

Only at the top landing Father says, very softly, "He liked it."

THE GENERAL

March 1811

I can smell the tanning vats from the courthouse. Most mornings, the winds carry the stench out to the lake, but today it rises up the slope, stronger as I approach. At the cabin above the sheds, the paint is peeling on the door. Inside, a baby cries. I hesitate, then knock.

"Fetch that door, will ya?"

"I got it, Ma."

The door opens with a wave of heat, along with the smells of cooking and baby pee. A tall girl looks down at me and smiles. Eli's smile — warm, friendly and full of straight teeth. She has his black hair and blue eyes. She wears a camisole, which is a garment Mother wears beneath her blouses, but Mother doesn't look like this. One strap has slipped and her collarbones are bare. She pulls a shawl up over her shoulders.

"You're little Jakie." I don't like being called "little" or "Jakie," but at least she knows who I am. "I'm Mina." She nods for me to come in. "It's Eli's friend,

Ma," she yells into the house. "The one what nearly drowned?" A thunder of little feet and two boys stare up at me from the level of the girl's hips. "This here's Jed and here's Benj'min."

Benjamin clings to his sister's skirt, and jams his other thumb into his mouth. Jed offers two roughly carved wooden shapes, one painted red, one blue. "You wanna play soldiers?" he asks. "You can be the lobster backs." He stabs the red figure with the blue one, and it clatters to the floor.

A blanket strung across the other end of the room swings open and a tall woman enters in her wooden shoes. Her blouse is loosened to nurse her baby.

"The Gibson boy?" she says. "That a fact."

Where should I look? I raise my eyes up to Mrs. McCabe's face. After our baby is born, will Mother wander around the house like this?

"Ain't you the purdiest little feller," she says. "Take a load off your feet."

"I can't stay, Mrs. McCabe. I want Eli to come with me to see the General."

"Well! Ain't that a fine, fine thing." A *fahn fahn thayng.* "Boys, your brother's gonna meet a general." She says it *gin'rul.*

"General Washington?" asks Jed.

Mina cuts in. "Eli ain't fit to meet no general, Mama. He's in the vat shed." She winks at me and pinches her nose.

As I approach the building at the bottom of the street, I know she's right. The place smells worse than a pigsty after the rain. I push open the door and the stench nearly makes me gag. Eli stands at a big wooden vat, holding a long stick in both hands while he stirs. He doesn't turn around.

"This batch is done-near ready, Pa."

I don't answer.

He turns his head and he sees me. His mouth opens in surprise. He drops his stick into the vat. His expression changes to horror and disgust — but not at me. He says a word I'm not allowed to say — maybe out of frustration, or maybe just stating what's inside that vat.

Father has a book by an Italian who says that hell has many different circles for bad people, and the worst one is supposed to be very cold. Well, I'm used to cold. It's not so bad. Much worse would be a place made up of the awful muck inside that vat. It looks like the pit at the bottom of our outhouse — all the poop and piss — only everything is mixed together like it was porridge. Half-sunken, like drowned men in a swamp, are big swaths of hide. And floating on top, but with one end buried in the mash, is Eli's stick.

He plunges his hand in and grabs the stick. Then both hands. But the mash sucks at the stick. Eli pulls and pulls, but he can't break it free.

"Quick!" Eli says. "Before it sinks."

I hesitate only a moment, then I reach down and grab.

Don't think about the hot, squishy feel. Just pull! Slowly. So slowly. It's moving upward. The tip of the handle clears. It drips with the brown-grey sludge.

Pull harder. Together. Now I realize that this is not just a stick. It's a wooden paddle that splatters big gobs when it clears the sludge. We both let go and it clatters to the floor. Eli and I crash to the ground with our backs against the wall. He looks at me and grins. I'm soaked with sweat on the inside of my clothes; sprayed with stink on the outside.

"Thanks."

I nod. I prepared a little speech in my head. I was going to tell Eli about how it didn't matter to me that his grandfather fought for George Washington. I was going to tell him that he is my best friend and the past and the war don't matter. But I've forgotten all of that now.

"Eli, I want you to come with me to see the General." I expect him to make objections. But he surprises me.

"When?"

My hands are covered with muck and I don't see any rags around so I scrape them against the floorboards.

"Not today — that's for sure."

He looks at me, puzzled. "Why not?"

* * *

The McCabes know as much about scrubbing clean as they do about making leather. And that's a lot. I stand in a tub in front of their fireplace, nearly naked in front of everyone while Mrs. McCabe scrubs me with lye soap. Mina grins at me. When I blush, it's not just the face that turns red.

"What's that?" she says.

I am squeezing my medicine bundle as tightly as little Benjamin squeezes Mina's hand.

"It's a gift."

"Can I see?"

Eli is waiting for his turn to step into the tub. "That there's Injun medicine. Jake don't let nobody touch it."

She looks at her brother and lifts her chin. "He'll let me," and she turns her eyes back on me.

With both hands I raise the cord over my head and pass it to her. "Just don't open it up. Please."

I don't know why I want to keep secret what is inside the medicine bag — some tobacco, a purple stone, the claw of a mountain lion. And something I added last week: a folded-up newspaper story. But the contents are mine and not meant for others to see.

"Aw, you're keeping big secrets, little Jakie?"

She is going to open it! I feel worse than if they

had suddenly asked me to strip off my remaining undershorts.

"Don't . . . Please . . . "

She looks at me and stops. Passes it back. "So, when's your pa taking you to see the General?"

I look to Eli. "I want to go with Eli. Just the two of us. No adults."

"Your pa won't mind?"

I don't reply. Father wants us to thank the General, but I think Eli and I should go on our own. Once you get grown-ups talking together, we boys don't count for much.

"Father says we're old enough to see him by ourselves." This seems like a small lie, but it turns my guts. Then the talk moves on to something else and I think: It works. Tell a little white lie and you can save yourself a lot of explaining.

The door opens and I shiver as the cold air rushes in. Mr. McCabe stands at the entrance. He's a huge man, big and round as a cannonball and every bit as hard. Beside him, Eli's mother seems slender and elegant. The two young boys rush to him and he lifts them up, one on each forearm.

"We have company, Cornelius," Mrs. McCabe says.

"You're the Gibson boy, ain't ya. Pleased to meet."

"Jake's gonna take me to see the General," says Eli, and his father's face clouds.

"You tell him," he says in a deep voice, "stay outta my life. I'll stay outta his."

I've seen Eli's father from a distance. Up close, he doesn't look nearly as fierce.

There's something I need to ask. Do I dare?

"Mr. McCabe? Why won't you swear the oath of allegiance?"

Eli stares at me like I've just left a gate open and all the pigs have escaped from the sty. Mr. McCabe narrows his eyes and studies me carefully.

"No king owns me," Mr. McCabe growls. "He don't own this land. It belongs to the people."

I nod my head as if I understand, but I don't. And I can't stop myself from asking, "But didn't you know the rules when you came?"

"Listen, young feller, you're a friend of my boy and you done all right by him. But I'll tell you this. I ain't indebted to no king. He ain't given me a cent, and I bought this property with the money what I brought from the States." He pauses to let that sink in. "Sooner or later, we'll all be part of the Republic, and we'll all be better for it."

I suck in my breath. Is this treason?

I return home that night and I don't tell Mother and Father that I've been to the McCabes'. I don't tell them that Eli and I plan to see General Brock tomorrow. I certainly don't tell them that I stood half-naked in the middle of the McCabe house. And above all, I don't tell them what Mr. McCabe thinks. They might never let me see Eli again.

* * *

The next morning, the sun shines strong enough to turn snow to slush. We three head up King Street, Ginger carrying her tail high, Eli even jumpier than Ginger. We're going to see the most famous man in all of Upper Canada. The man who saved my life.

"What made you change your mind?"

"'Bout what?"

I look sideways at him. He really doesn't remember that he didn't want to come?

"You were worried about your father."

"Reckon I should set things right — if I can."

"You?"

"Corn, Pa ain't gonna do nothing. Someone's got to say his piece."

I pick up a stick from the side of the road and slash at the air.

"He should just swear the oath."

"They should just leave him alone."

Eli finds a stick as well. We slash at each other — parry, thrust. Ginger leaps up to play. We fight our way past the courthouse and pause to wave to Mr. McKenney. You know spring is on its way when he sits on the steps to enjoy the sun.

Eli lowers his sword. "Them big humbugs what got

all the power and money — Old Man Dunwoody and all." Eli nods up the road where the Dunwoodys' brick house stands at the corner. "They ain't gonna leave Pa alone nohow." I follow him up the road and he continues, "They want him out for militia duty."

"Everyone's got to be in the militia, Eli. Once you're sixteen."

"Yeah . . . "

"Four more years. I can't wait!" I raise my stick and pretend to shoot a musket at the Dunwoody house. Eli throws his across the snake-rail fence and Ginger yelps as she chases after it. I shoulder my stick and march. Everything looks quiet there. Too bad. I'd love to have William and Henry see this — watch us parade to our own personal meeting with General Brock.

As we pass, I glance up at the windows in the top floor. The curtains part. Good. They'll see us. If I were younger, I'd stick out my tongue.

But it's not William up there.

It's Mina.

What's she doing in the Dunwoody house? Upstairs, no less.

She stares out to the lake, then down at us. And when she sees me watching her, she pulls the curtains closed again.

Did that really happen? The curtains are so still now. I say nothing to Eli, and he marches ahead with

Ginger. I hurry to catch up, but look back at the upper-floor window.

The curtains part again. This time it is William, and he looks straight down at us. He smiles like a cat who caught the mouse. I trip and catch my balance and, when I glance back, he laughs and tugs the curtains closed.

What have I just seen? Was she really there? With *him!*

I stumble on the stairs of the General's headquarters. Eli pounds on the door and it swings open. We're almost bowled over by a lieutenant who pushes past, mounts a waiting horse, and canters down the road toward the fort. Another officer — an ensign — thrusts past us on his way in.

"Hey! You two! What do you want?"

A chevroned sleeve blocks our passage. I look up. A big corporal stands in the doorway.

"We want to see the General . . . sir."

"Out with you."

"We're the ones what he fished out of the river," says Eli. "Well, my friend is. But I reckon he saved me too . . . sir."

The corporal looks at us more carefully. "I'm no sir."

I follow his glance into the dark interior. At the other end of the hallway, the door opens and the ensign strides back out and rushes past us.

"Wait in there," the corporal says. "And not a peep from either of you."

There's not much furniture in the General's lobby. The room smells of fresh wax. I fidget beside Eli on a bench. We're both restless as puppies.

I take the plunge. "Did you see that?" I whisper.

"What?"

"Back there. The Dunwoody house. Your si— "

The corporal knocks softly on a door and slips inside. A voice snaps, "You are drunk, sir!" It's a loud, booming voice — a voice to be heard above the din of battle, even without shouting.

Eli giggles. That corporal hadn't seemed drunk to me.

I begin again, whispering to Eli, "Did you see the window?"

But before Eli can answer, another voice behind the wall replies, "You may be right, General. Later I shall be sober, and my arguments will still be as valid."

I know that voice — a good-natured, rolling Irish accent. Then the door closes again.

But the General raises his voice still louder and we hear it clearly through the walls. "You, sir, will do what is expected of a good Briton in a time of peril."

The Irish voice rises too, but keeps its good humour. "Begging your pardon, General — and no disrespect — but the last time I checked, Parliament is still independent of the Crown. Even in this province."

Eli whispers, "Maybe we should come back later?"

"There is no later," I hiss back — not with General Brock.

The General lowers his voice, but the words are crisp and strong, with that English accent, rich as ripe fruit. "We will discuss this further, sir. In York. Before the next Session."

"As you wish, General. Thank you, Corporal, I can find my way out."

The door opens and the silhouette of a big man stands against the sunlight.

"Young Jacob Gibson! Bless my soul, wonderful to see you here. Where's your father?"

Mr. Willcocks steps forward, a bit unsteady and holding out his walking stick to keep his balance. He gives us a broad smile. I smell rum on his breath. He turns to Eli. "And this, I believe, is our young hero. I know your father. Capital man. Salt of the earth. Well, must be on my way." He turns to me. "Tell your mother I shan't be late for dinner this time."

Eli and I watch as he disappears out into the street. The door closes and the lobby is dark again.

"The window. Did you see? Your sister?"

Eli looks at me funny.

"At the *Dunwoody* house. Upstairs. With William."

What do I expect? Maybe he'll get mad at me again.

He looks down at the floor.

"But she can't . . . " I plead. "She can't be on their side. Can she?"

He doesn't look up.

"It's beyond figuring," he says. "With girls." He nods at the crack between the pine planks. "A penny for who gets it first, Jake."

"Eli . . . "

"Two cents, then."

"Eli!"

But there's no stopping him. He leans over and a small gob of spit drops from his mouth and splats beside the crack.

"Dang," he says. "Your turn."

"This is the General's house!"

He shrugs. "We'll clean up." And he scuffs the spit into the paint with his boot.

The door opens. "The General will receive you now," the corporal says.

Receive us. That's what generals do, I guess. They don't see us, or talk to us, or invite us in. They *receive* us as if we were a shipment sent from a distant place.

I follow Eli as he saunters into the room. A big window faces out onto the market square. In front of it, General Brock sits at his desk, writing. He does not look up. The corporal closes the door as he leaves. Two wooden chairs wait empty by the hearth where a fire flickers. A clock ticks on the mantle. The General's quill scratches. He dips it into the ink without raising his head.

General Brock is a big man who fills his chair. His head is huge and, from where I stand, I see that his hair is thinning on top. Most of the time he wears a bicorn hat, and even when he's not, he's so tall that people don't see the top of his head. How many know what I know? General Brock is balding.

He dips his quill again and signs with a flourish. "Porter!" he calls with that ripe accent. *Poah-tah* . . . He makes no effort to raise his voice, but I think he's loud enough to be heard throughout the house.

The corporal steps in. "Sir!"

"This for Governor Gore," the General says. "Mr. Macdonnell to arrange."

General Brock folds the paper and passes it to Corporal Porter. Only then does he look at us. His eyes are cool and aloof.

I stiffen to attention.

"The boys from the river." He rises to his feet. He keeps on rising. I've never seen anyone so big.

Am I supposed to shake the General's hand? Many English people don't like to shake hands. I give a little bow.

"How do you do," he says as he nods his head.

He turns to Eli. "And you are . . . " He searches his memory for the name.

"McCabe, General. Eli McCabe." Eli thrusts out

his hand. The General simply nods as he listens to Eli's accent.

"How do you do," he says. And then he smiles at us. I wish Father were here. "You are a strong and determined young boy, Master McCabe. You wouldn't let go, even when we had Master Gibson out of the water."

Eli blushes.

"And you're looking much better, Master Gibson. I'm pleased that you're recovering." He raises one eyebrow. "But your father has not accompanied you?"

What do I say now? "He wanted me to thank you. On my own." I stand ramrod straight.

The General studies me. "Stand easy, Master Gibson. Your father is with the Lincolns, I believe? He fought in the late rebellion. A ranger, I understand."

"Yes, sir."

"I know him. A good soldier."

"Yes, sir." Father should hear this! "General, I want to thank you . . . Eli and I want to thank you . . . for saving my life . . . our lives."

He gazes at me with calm eyes. It's the way my father looks when he candles the eggs to see inside the shells.

"I trust, young man, that you've learned a lesson about not going onto the river."

"He did it for me, sir," Eli blurts. "They dared me to — Junior and Lug . . . I mean, William Dunwoody and Henry Ecker. To walk clear across the river, and then they changed it to my pa's tannery. They was trying to be mean to me, but Jake here, he showed 'em. Showed 'em real good."

General Brock turns that egg-candling stare onto Eli. "Your father has recently arrived here? McCabe the tanner?"

"Uh, yes . . . sir . . . "

Does General Brock know everything that happens in this town? Eli flushes with pride and he stands taller too. But the General turns and pulls a folio from the wooden tray. He studies a paper inside.

He turns his eyes back to Eli, and he says in a very cold voice — a bayonet voice, "Your father has not sworn."

"N-no, sir."

Even General Brock knows that Eli's pa hasn't sworn allegiance to the British Crown. He scans down the paper and mutters as if talking to himself, "Hasn't mustered for militia duty."

"I just wanted to explain . . . "

"If it were up to me," the General says as if he hasn't heard, "there would be no excuses."

"Yes, sir," Eli mumbles.

The General continues to study the newspaper. "Enough of this nonsense about paying paltry fines. Evict them from the colonies."

Eli and I say nothing.

The General glances up as if he'd forgotten we were here.

"That will be all," he says.

"Thank you . . . again . . . for saving my life, I mean."

The General nods.

Outside, Ginger waits for us. The snow is bright and we shield our eyes.

Eli is as pale as the winter sky. "That didn't go so well," he says.

"What are you going to tell your father?"

"Dunno. Best say nothing, I reckon. What about yours?"

I stop dead in the middle of the street. I don't know! I didn't even tell him that I was coming to see the General. Now if I tell him, I'll also have to say that the General is angry with Eli's father. And then he might not let me see Eli anymore.

I thought I would come home and announce that I had gone to thank the General. Mother and Father would be so proud of me. Now it must be kept secret.

And then something else occurs to me.

"What's wrong, Jake?"

"I can't."

"Can't what?"

"Keep it secret. Mr. Willcocks is coming for dinner. Tonight."

"Will he tell your ma and pa?"

"Mr. Willcocks? He feasts on gossip."

"Corn, Jake. Ask him not to say nothing."

I'm not sure he'd do it. I'm not even sure if Mr. Willcocks *can* keep a secret.

"What are you going to do, Jake?"

I don't have an answer. Not yet.

"You better tell me what you tell him." Eli shakes his head. "We gotta keep our stories straight."

"Meet me before sunrise. At the lighthouse."

BLOOD BROTHERS

March 1811

I keep piling up the list of what I have not told Mother and Father.

I have not told them that William and Henry pick on Eli.

I have not told them that Eli thinks George Washington is a hero and that Father was on the side of the traitors.

I have not told them that Eli's father has not sworn allegiance, and that he thinks we'd be better off as part of the United States.

I know I won't tell them that I saw Mina McCabe upstairs at the Dunwoody house.

And now this — that we went to see General Brock and he's upset about Eli's father.

Children should be seen and not heard: that's the rule when my parents have guests for dinner. I sure hope so tonight!

The dinner guests arrive: Mr. and Mrs. Lawe, Mr. and Mrs. McRoberts. No sign of Mr. Willcocks.

Maybe he won't come after all. That would be good.

But just as we sit down to table, Cathleen answers the door and in he sweeps like a blizzard of frock coat, walking stick and scarf.

"Sorry, dear people. Ever so sorry. Had to get out the next edition. The *Guardian* waits for no man — or dinner party. Everything aright? Right as roosters!"

Mother calls Mr. Willcocks her "pet bachelor." Every family should have one, she says: an unmarried man to provide with home-cooked meals and a sense of family. In return, Mr. Willcocks charms the guests.

He always has so much to talk about — politics in York, and the war in Europe. Meeting Eli and me at the General's may be beneath his notice.

No such luck. Halfway through the soup course, he beams down the table at me and calls, "And you, Master Jacob! What did General Brock have to say to you today?"

All conversation halts. Even Cathleen pauses on her way out to the kitchen.

"Oh," says Mr. Willcocks, "did I say something?"

Father pierces me with his look. "You talked to the General? Today?"

Mr. Willcocks tries to rescue me. "Oh, I'm only assuming, Robert. We saw each other near Government House."

But Father won't be distracted. "You spoke with General Brock? And you didn't tell us?"

Seen and not heard! But I have to say something now. "I thanked him. For rescuing me."

Mother intervenes. "That was very thoughtful of you, dear. But you might have told us beforehand."

"And afterwards." Father frowns.

Mrs. Lawe adds, "Well, what did he say?"

Now I'm in for it. Faces stare. Cathleen puts the soup tureen down on the sideboard and listens.

"He told us to stay off the ice."

"That's all?"

"And he says he knows you, Father. He says you're a good soldier."

I hope that the conversation will pass on to something else.

But Mr. Willcocks adds, "And what about your young friend — the McCabe boy?"

"Eli went too?" Mother asks. At the head of the table, Father puts down his napkin and scrutinizes me.

"He said that Eli was very strong." This is true. "He asked if his father was the tanner." Uh-oh, I'm getting too close. I glance at the candles, then the doorway, then the picture of the Duke of Marlborough on the wall. "In fact," I continue, "General Brock wants to give Eli a medal for bravery."

All of them lean forward and look down the table at me.

"Splendid!" Mr. Willcocks says. "What a wonderful story for the newspaper."

What do I do now?

"We should wait. Eli wants to keep it a secret. Until he has the medal. As a surprise. For his parents."

The adults nod in agreement.

"You'll let me know, young Jacob," says Mr. Willcocks. "As soon as we can publish. In the meantime, I'll inquire with the General."

"I think General Brock wants to keep it a secret too. Until it's . . . it's . . . "

"Official?" Mr. Willcocks offers.

One more lie to add to the list. How am I ever going to keep track?

* * *

For as long as I can remember, I have wanted to stay with the men after we've finished eating and the ladies have retired to the parlour. Cathleen serves tea for the women, and the men bring out pipes and a decanter of port. And me? I'm always sent upstairs to bed. This has never seemed fair.

But tonight, I'm more than happy to get away before I say anything else stupid. I only pretend to go to bed. I take my usual place by the railing at the top of the stairs. After Cathleen has tended to the ladies, she brings me tea, with lots of milk and sugar. My fingers grip the warm china. In the past, I have listened out of curiosity. Tonight, I need to know whether Eli and I are in even more trouble than I imagine.

At first it's hard to hear, but as more port gets passed around the table, the men's voices grow louder.

"That boy of yours, Gibson, he's a bright and presentable lad."

Father says something that is too low to reach me.

"But the McCabe boy too!" says Mr. Lawe. "A medal! From the General himself!"

Mr. Willcocks's voice rises above the others. "Lads . . . lads, I wouldn't be holding up production of the newspaper for that story." The others fall silent. I squeeze my teacup tighter. "I think old McCabe is in too much trouble with the magistrate. With the General, too, most likely. Robert, has he shown up for militia drill?"

Father replies in his low voice. All I can make out is, " . . . rather pay the fine."

"There you have it!" Mr. Willcocks resumes. "A practical solution for McCabe and for the treasury. As long as he pays his two dollars, he doesn't need to train with the militia. But it's not over for our friend McCabe, you know."

And then Mr. Willcocks lowers his voice and says something I can't quite hear. Just a few words: " . . . evicted from the Canadas."

That's when my fingers tighten. The cup shoots out like the centre of a cooked onion. I scramble to catch the teacup but I miss, and it takes forever to tumble from the second floor. The china smashes onto the boards below with the sound of an axe blow, and the tea splashes as far as the wall.

I shoot to my feet.

At the bottom of the stairs, the parlour door opens. Cathleen rushes out, looks at the mess, then up the stairs at me.

Mother and our lady guests lean forward in their chairs and peer out.

Ginger wanders leisurely to lick up the spill.

Then the other door below swings wide. Father stands with his hands on his hips, and his boots crunch on shattered porcelain.

"Come down," he barks. "Now."

He waits before the door.

"I'm sorry, Father. I didn't mean to break it."

His voice is as deep as trouble. "Have you been spying?"

"I . . . I mean to say . . . " I hang my head. "Yes, sir."

I knew the day might come when I would be caught listening in.

Then another voice calls, "Has the boy been eaves-dropping? What a clever lad."

Mr. Willcocks joins my father, grinning at me.

Father glances behind me to Mother, and he nods to her. His eyes return to me. "Jacob," he says, "would you care to join us?"

"Yes, sir," I murmur. And I repeat more loudly, "Yes, sir!"

* * *

On the ridge above the lake, the lighthouse shines into the night. From the town, it seems to flash as regularly as a clock ticks. But it looks different nearer the tower. The beam circles slowly around in a wide arc. It points toward the lake, sweeping across big chunks of ice that float out there in the dark. When it swings back to the land, the light rushes in and out through the bare branches, boughs and trunks. Then everything is black once more.

What is out there in the forest? Not even Ginger dares to explore. She lies close to my feet on the frozen ground. Then she scrambles up, alert. She wags her tail. I hear footsteps, grinding on the gravel of the shoreline.

"That general?" Eli's voice calls in the darkness. "I don't think he likes me." His voice is too loud, too brave in this dark night. I can see his face in the moonlight. "What we gonna do, Jake? That there general and all them other men, they got it in for my pa."

I don't want to tell him that Father is among those who think the McCabes should not stay. The lighthouse beam sweeps across the fort on the other side of the river.

"Maybe he could swear the oath anyway, but cross his fingers?"

"Pa ain't like that. He stands by his word."

"It can't be that big a deal, Eli. It's not worth being thrown out of the province."

"What?"

"They're planning to throw you all out. Mr. Willcocks says so. Just swear the oath. Show up on the King's birthday. March with the militia. It's not too much."

"If there's a war, he'd have to fight for the King. He hates kings."

"Then why did he come?"

Eli shrugs. "Land's cheap, he says. Ain't got much taxes. He just wants to be left alone."

We're both looking down. "Maybe there won't be a war," I offer.

"Would he still have to swear allegiance?"

I don't know the answer. But there's something else that bothers me — about loyalty, allegiance.

"Eli, is your sister friends with . . . with William and Henry?"

Now it's Eli who looks across the water. "She says them boys is nice to her. Real nice."

"How can she be friends with them if they're so mean to us?"

"I promised her I wouldn't tell Ma and Pa. They'd be right vexed." He turns and looks at me. "Jake, you and me, we can't let none of this stand atwixt us."

"It's not going to, Eli."

"Not my pa and his oath. Not my sis and her boyfriends. Not King George and not even George Washington." The beam swings around before he says, "Jake, you and me's gotta stay together."

I nod.

"Promise me?"

And I say, "We could swear an oath too."

"You and me? We'd be like blood brothers." Then his voice rises. "That's it, Jake! Blood brothers. Ain't no one gonna split us apart."

"How do we do it?"

He thinks a moment, then pulls his pocket knife from his trousers. He opens it and draws the blade across his palm. He doesn't have to press hard. A line of dark blood oozes in the blade's trail.

We lean forward with our heads together. The mist of our breath mingles and rises in the still air.

"Now you." He passes me his knife.

It stings. Doesn't matter.

We face each other, each of us with our left hand cupped up, the palm slowly filling with blood. Some drops of blood — his or mine, I cannot tell — splat onto the frozen grass. Ginger comes to sniff.

"What now?" I ask.

He reaches out with his hand and I grasp it, thumb around thumb, fingers around wrist — the grip for arm wrestling. Blood trickles down my shirt cuff.

"We should say something," Eli says.

"All right. I, Jacob Robert Gibson . . . "

"I, Cornelius McCabe Junior . . . "

"Cornelius? Junior?"

"Just get on with it."

"Do solemnly swear . . . "

"Do solemnly swear . . . "

"That I will be a true and faithful friend to Eli McCabe . . . Uh, Cornelius McCabe Junior."

"That I will be a true and faithful friend to Jacob Gibson."

"I will love him like a brother."

"I will love him like a brother."

"And my true blood brother he will always be."

"And my true blood brother he will always be."

"So help me God."

"So help me God."

We stand silent.

"You're really good with words, Slim." *Slim.* He has given me a nickname. I like it.

"I guess we should make a secret society. We should have a name for it."

"What about . . . " He pauses. "The Lighthouse Society."

"The Friends of the Lighthouse."

"*Brothers* of the Lighthouse. Ain't no one gonna push us around. Not no bullies. Not no generals. No one."

I hand him back the knife.

"No, you keep it. It's yours now."

"You sure?" And then I realize. "Eli, I don't have anything to give you."

"That don't matter."

"I'll get you something. Something special. One of these days."

URINE WARS

July 1811

The hottest day of summer, when the cicadas whirr and the leaves turn their dull, silvery sides to the sun. On the lake, sails hang limp on the boats. Eli and I stir up little clouds of dust as we walk. Ginger can't be bothered to sniff along the roadway.

A day for swimming. We cut through the churchyard. I stop to pick some flowers. After a moment, Eli picks some too.

We walk in silence among the tombstones. Our town is new, and the stones are new too. On one grave, the dirt is piled high and no grass grows. I put the flowers on top of the tombstone. So does Eli. We sit down cross-legged.

The sun beats down brightly on the stone, which stands rigid and straight:

Sacred to the memory of Jane Gibson
Beloved wife of Robert Gibson
Born Aberdour, Scotland, November 17, 1775
Died Newark, U.C., June 4, 1811

&

Charlotte Gibson
Born June 3, 1811, Died June 5, 1811

Nearby there are other stones, smaller, as if in hopes that each one will be the last. They carry the names of a brother and sisters I never got to know.

William Gibson, September 10, 1802
Mary Ellen Gibson, March 6, 1805
Elizabeth Gibson, January 25, 1807

After a while, Eli says, "If you read a grave, Jake, the words is real simple, but the stories is real strategies."

I pick grass at my feet. "It's not tragedy."

"Corn, Slim." He sounds offended — like it's up to him to defend Mother and Charlotte, and William, Mary and Elizabeth. "What could be sadder than that?"

I won't argue, but in school, Dominie Burns teaches that tragedy comes from something bad in your character — a flaw that makes you reach beyond yourself and you're struck down by Fate. That's not my mother. That was not my brother and sist—

I let the tears trickle down my cheeks but say nothing as I study the grass. I glance up and Eli is watching me, a straw of grass in his lips. He looks away and starts to sing under his breath. *"Boney was a general . . . "*

He waits for me to join, but I will not.

He continues, *"Away hey ya . . . "*

A butterfly lands on my boot. It waves its wings a couple of times, then we both watch it flitter away.

"A *randy dandy general* . . . " His voice still soft.

An ant carries a dead spider up the slope of the turned earth. On top of the tombstone, the flowers have been baked limp and lifeless.

After a pause, he sings almost in a whisper, "*John France-wah* . . . "

I can smell the aroma of Eli's pouch — or maybe it's the reek of the tannery just beyond the trees. I hope that's what I'm smelling. It's a terrible thing to think of Mother and Charlotte below the ground. How long will it take before the coffin rots and the earth and the worms and the ants get in? Can you smell that?

The deerskin of my medicine bundle is smooth and shiny with sweat. The sweat has been rubbed in deeply. By my fingers. And others before me.

There was an odour like swamp water in the room the day they set Mother and Charlotte out on the table. They lay there in their caskets, and the curtains were closed and candles were lit in the middle of a summer day.

Father and I sat in that room, sometimes alone, sometimes with visitors. Eli and his family came, and Mina held Benjamin on her lap. Mrs. McCabe held the baby. Eli was lucky to have brothers and sisters and babies who sometimes squawked, sometimes gurgled, and sometimes slept. Charlotte was sleeping in that little wooden box and she looked as sweet and as innocent as any baby I'd ever seen, but she wasn't going to wake up.

Then the time came to say goodbye and Father held me by the shoulders while I touched Mother's hands and kissed her forehead. Her skin was so cold and I thought, "This isn't your skin. You're not my mother," but I kept looking at her eyes, hoping they'd open and she would say in that warm, low voice, "It's all right, little man."

But those eyes did not open, and they put a cover over the casket and then over Charlotte's little box. The others carried them up to the church and Father and I followed.

The smell followed me out of the parlour, into the afternoon light. It lingered on the black crepe and on my skin. Candles and flowers and the odour of something that had once been alive and sweet but was neither of those things now.

Ginger comes up to lick the tears from my face and I rise to my feet and head toward the trees. I wipe my nose on my sleeve, and that's when I notice it again.

"You smell that?" I ask Eli.

"Smell what?"

I shake my head. No sense asking Eli.

* * *

"So . . . Jake . . . Is your pa ever gonna remarry?"

I give Eli a sour look.

"I don't mean tomorrow or nothing. But some-time?"

"Father would never marry someone else. He loved Mother too much."

Cooler air comes up from the lake with a promise of cold water against my skin. Maybe I'll swim right across the lake. Swim until I forget everything.

"Can't go around with no ma, Jake. And your pa, he's gotta have a wife. Otherwise he'd get ornery and maybe a bit cuckoo. Like Mr. Willcocks."

I just keep walking.

"My pa, he says women's a civilating influence."

Father was from the Mohawk Valley. It was Mother who taught him how to use *who* and *whom*.

That stench is getting stronger again.

"You smell it now?"

If it were coming from the McCabe tannery, I'd know exactly what the smell was. But it's not coming from there. In fact, it's coming from the courthouse.

On a hot day like this, you'd expect Mr. McKenney to stay in the coolness of the jail cells, playing cards with a prisoner, if he has one. But he's out on the front steps in the blazing heat, stomping about the porch on his wooden leg, swishing a mop.

He shades his eyes as he squints up the road at us. "There ye be! Get over here, Eli McCabe. Right now!"

Usually Mr. McKenney is happy to see Eli. Often I come with him to collect the contents of the piss-pots from the jail cells, and sometimes he delivers Mr. McKenney a jug of his pa's homemade alcohol.

But Mr. McKenney certainly is not happy to see Eli now. "I said get over here!" he orders.

Eli and I look up from the bottom step. The smell is so bad that not even the soapy water can cover it. Shards of broken pottery lie around the steps.

"You made the mess. Now you clean it up." Mr. McKenney thrusts the mop toward us.

Eli scratches his nose. "Clean up what?"

I whisper to him, "You still don't smell it?" I nudge him and point around at the shattered clay. "Aren't those the pots you collect piss with?"

Someone has brought a jug of urine and smashed it against the courthouse.

"When you've finished here," Mr. McKenney says, "you can scrub the rest of the town. Reverend Addison wants to see you. And Dominie Burns. So does Corporal Porter. Every public building in town smells of piss and we know you did it."

"But he didn't do it," I say. "Honest. I've been with Eli the whole time."

Mr. McKenney casts his good eye on me. At the Battle of Saratoga, he lost one eye and one leg and had part of his chin shot away. He looks fierce even when he's not angry.

"Tell it to Magistrate Dunwoody." That's William's father. "I should lock you up right now. Then we'll see what His Honour has to say about it."

"I didn't do nothing wrong," says Eli, "but I'll help you clean it up."

"Me too," I chip in.

"And later on," Eli adds, "I think my pa's got a little present for you. New batch. Fresh last week."

Mr. McKenney retreats inside and we work in the heat, Eli with the mop and I on my hands and knees with a brush. Ginger watches from the shade.

"You reckon they could do that?" says Eli. "Throw us in jail? No trial? No nothing?"

I shake my head. "I don't think so."

"And Junior's pa to judge us?" Eli continues. "Wouldn't happen back home. But here? With King George and all?"

What to say? It's too hot to talk. Eli's pa finally swore the oath of allegiance, but can they still throw him out of the country?

They say war is coming. Magistrate Dunwoody wants to jail suspicious persons. Without trial if need be. In his newspaper, Mr. Willcocks writes that this is a bad idea.

By the time we've finished, my shirt is soaked. Sweat trickles down Eli's face, but he hasn't lost his smile. Now the courthouse smells of soap and sun, and we borrow Mr. McKenney's brush, mop and pail and head back to the English church. The brush rattles in the bottom of the wooden bucket. I shoulder the mop like a musket. The water drips a trail in the dust.

"Not how I hoped to spend the afternoon," I say.

"Rather be swimming."

Our shadows march in the road before us. We used to be smaller and skinnier together. He's a bit taller now and broader across the shoulders than me.

"Who do you think did it?"

Eli looks across at me and his smile fades for just a moment. "Someone's out to get us," he says.

* * *

At the English church, the Reverend Mr. Addison gives us a drink of water and fills the bucket. In the shimmering heat, a woman in a white bonnet walks toward us. She swings her hips and hikes up her skirts. It's not a woman. It's a girl.

"Pa's gonna whup you good, Eli," Mina says. "They say you done stank up this here whole town."

"I didn't do it."

"I believe you," she sighs. "I reckon someone else did. Come on. I'll give you a hand."

Mina hitches her skirts even higher to scrub. Her legs are very long and white above the calves, but her bare feet and ankles are brown as walnuts. I try to focus on my work.

With three people and a dog, it doesn't take long to scour the smell of pee from the stones. Maybe it would take even less time without the dog. Ginger thinks her job is to add more for us to clean up. When we've finished the English church, we head up the street toward Government House. Mina and Ginger move on ahead.

I whisper to Eli, "Your sister knows who did this?" He says nothing. "Whose side is she on?" He shakes his head and won't meet my eyes.

At Government House, Corporal Porter tells us General Brock is not in town. But the corporal's happy to have us wash away the smell. We fill our buckets from the pump in the market square. Mina joins us when we splash our heads under the water. The sun sparkles on the water droplets on her skin. Her blouse sticks to the contours of her collarbones. Eli and I work the mops, and Mina takes the scrub brush. Ginger finds a spot in the shade beside her.

Voices call from across the street.

"Things must be getting tough in the tannery business."

"Scrubbing piss off the streets?"

William and Henry watch us from the corner at the Dunwoody house. They cross the road. William's shirt is white and crisp as a summer cloud.

Ginger rises and growls. Eli and I stop mopping, but Mina keeps her eyes down, studying the soapsuds on the stones. She reaches over and grips Ginger around the shoulders.

William sneers, "Well, McCabe, it looks like *urine* trouble now."

"You know what they say," Henry adds, "*urine* or you're out."

"Hey, Henry, what did the jailor say to the tanner's son?"

"I don't know, William. What did he say?"

"Piss . . . off!"

I mutter, "You boys seem to think you're pretty funny."

They smirk, and William says, "Gibson, I'm surprised to find you here with Turd Boy. Thought you were in mourning."

"Sorry about your mother," Henry adds.

"Yes," William adds, "terribly sad, really."

"She was a gracious lady."

"Yes. Quite the lady."

"You going to help or not?" I reply.

William scoffs. "Help? We *hire* help."

"You two seem to know a lot about all of this," I say.

"Where'd you get all that pee anyway?" asks Eli. He swishes his mop in the soapy water. "Seems like a terrible waste."

"You ought to mind your Ps and Qs, McCabe," snorts Henry.

William steps forward to where Mina holds Ginger back. She won't look up. "And here's Miss Mina," he says. "Hello, Miss Mina. Don't you have better things to do than clean — "

"Leave my sister alone," growls Eli. And he flicks his mop up, sending a spray of dirty water over the two boys.

"Hey!" shouts Henry. He takes a step toward Eli and raises his fists.

I flick my sopping mop. Another arc of smelly water showers on them.

"Stop that!" William cowers from the spray.

Eli and I plunge our mops in the buckets again. We hurl another load.

Mina lets Ginger go and the boys turn and run. Mina throws her brush. She has a good arm. The brush arches end over end, spraying droplets in the sun. It hits William between the shoulder blades.

Ginger barks after them until they retreat to the safety of the Dunwoody house.

Mina stands beside us. "Well, I guess they ain't gonna help us," she says. She returns to her scrubbing, and I think I hear her singing under her breath.

TACTICAL RAID

August 1811

"Gibson!"

Uh-oh, William Dunwoody.

I haven't seen him since the encounter with the soapy water. I'm at the wharves alone. No Ginger here to protect me. There are no other boys in sight — not even the dockers. I pretend I haven't heard, turn and walk toward land.

"Gibson, wait up!"

What does he want with me? It can't be good. I look up to the Navy Hall and the fort. Was it only last winter that I stood in the snow on that hillside, so proud that I'd been chosen first?

The dock is crowded with crates and sacks. Big men push wheelbarrows and the planks creak under the weight. Can I make a run for it?

I skitter around the men working the block and tackle, and one curses at me to get out of the way.

But there, on the shore, Henry stands between me and the warehouses.

Maybe I could get away across the decks of the ships. But the biggest longshoreman of them all straightens his back from where he hauls a sack out of the hold. He glances down the dock toward William and nods that he understands. He steps toward me and holds out his massive arms to bar my way.

Just my luck. This is one of the Dunwoody boats.

Dive into the river? They'd never follow me. Would they?

Last winter I would have given anything to be counted among their friends. Now I'm scared of them.

"Gibson, will you hold on for a moment."

I won't be scared. I take a deep breath. The air stinks of hemp rope and tar. Henry's footsteps clomp on the planks. "We just want to talk," he says.

They stand so tall on either side of me.

William nods for me to follow and heads down the dock. "Gibson, I've been meaning to talk to you." With every step we get closer to shore. "We're sorry about that last incident." *They're* sorry? "Somehow you and I've gone wrong with each other."

My feet touch the dirt of the road. I take deep breaths. We weave our way through the longshore-men as they load wagons with hogsheads and sacks.

"Leave me alone. Leave Eli alone too."

They exchange glances. "Hear us out, Gibson," William says. "Why don't we get a cider at the Yellow Tavern? Or better yet, would you like to join us for tea? Mrs. Hawkins makes wonderful crumpets."

Cider? Tea?

I've never been inside the Dunwoody house. Mr. Willcocks says the crumpets there are the best.

"What's this all about, William Dunwoody?"

William takes my arm, but in a friendly way. He matches my pace. "You're a good fellow, Gibson. You come from a good family."

Henry adds, "I don't know why you're hanging around with a troublemaker like McCabe."

"*You* tried to get Eli in trouble."

"There's a reason why we're tough on McCabe," says William.

"I think his father's a spy," Henry says.

I stop and ponder this a moment. "He can't be a spy. He wouldn't draw attention to himself."

"Exactly!" says Henry. "How can you trust someone who took so long to swear allegiance? He still won't show up for militia day. Not even on the King's birthday."

I glare. "My father wasn't there either." Mother died on the King's birthday. No parades, fireworks and dance parties for us.

Henry blushes and looks down. "Yes. Sorry. Terrible thing, really."

"What do you two want?"

William draws a deep breath before he says, "Let's get back on the right foot, Gibson. You've got pluck,

I'll say that for you. When you're older, maybe you'll serve with us in the flank companies."

"What are flank companies?"

"You haven't heard? Something new that General Brock wants to introduce."

"And it's that rascal Joe Willcocks," Henry sneers, "who's trying to stop him."

"They're special militia units, Gibson. Extra training. Almost like regular soldiers."

"Why would *anyone* vote against that?" Henry asks. Then he adds, "You know what I think? I think Willcocks is being paid by the Americans to stir up trouble." He looks at William. "You can't trust the Irish."

William puts a hand on his friend's arm, and Henry falls silent. "We need to root out the traitors, Gibson. Men who won't show up on militia day. Politicians who get in the way when we prepare for war. I think you would agree."

"I . . . I haven't thought about it."

"Well, do think about it, Gibson. And come talk to us."

"Sure you won't come for tea?"

"I . . . I have other places I need to be."

"Some other time, then."

I stand watching them as they make their way back to the wharves and the ships. Another boat is sailing up the river and preparing to dock. There's a big world out there, and I don't understand it. I don't even understand what's going on in my town.

The other place I need to be is Eli's house. Wait until he hears this!

Down where the river enters the lake, the McCabes' mill stands next door to the tannery shed. Rather than the stench of the vat, it smells of the wood they crush to dye the leather.

"We could join the flank companies," I tell Eli.

"What's flank companies?" He remains focused on scraping the flesh off a hide stretched on a frame.

"Special militia. Almost like real soldiers."

"Really?"

"They're going to get extra training."

"That would be fun!" Eli has forgotten the hide now.

"But we'd probably have to serve alongside William and Henry."

Eli pays this no mind. He raises the knife to his face and sights along it, pretending to fire a musket. "*Fssshht. Bam!*" He looks at me. "Do you reckon we'd get to train inside the fort?"

"Maybe we'd get to shoot the cannons too," I offer. I pretend to light a touch hole. "Fire! *Ka-boom!*"

The mill door swings open and Mina stands in the light, her fist on her hip. "You two's playing like little boys. Meanwhile them two's out to get you again."

We don't have to ask her which two she means.

"You still passing time with them?"

"Maybe I am, maybe I ain't. You just tend to your-self."

"What's going on?" I ask.

"They're storing up pee. Jugs of it — just like they musta done afore."

"How *you* know?"

"Never you mind, little brother. Just be glad I know. And gladder I'm telling *you*."

I look to Eli, then to Mina. "What should we do?"

* * *

The next morning, the sun peeks over the American fort. Our steps leave a trail through the dew. At the snake-rail fence behind the Dunwoody house, I point out our tracks.

"Maybe we should wait until the dew's gone," I whisper.

Eli thinks a moment. "Move now, when the sun's in their eyes."

Mina jabs her brother. "You two waiting for a invite or something?"

She climbs the fence and leads the way around the vegetable garden. From the brick house across the yard comes the clatter of pots and dishes and the smell of wood smoke — Mr. and Mrs. Hawkins up early, tending to the Dunwoody household before anyone else is awake. We reach the stable and Eli shoves the big sliding door aside a crack and we all squeeze through.

The stable smells of horses, straw and manure. Shafts of sun streak through the knotholes, and hay dust floats in the beams of light. My nose itches.

Horse stalls stretch into the darkness. The Dunwoodys boast the finest carriage horse in the county. His name is Belvedere. They have three excellent riding horses too: Shadrach, Meshach and Abednego. I scrape oats from the floor to give them to Belvedere. Eli offers Abednego hay. My nose starts to run and I blow quietly into my handkerchief.

From the hay crib at the far end of the stalls, Mina hisses, "C'mon!" She scrambles over the rails into the hay, and I catch a glimpse of her lean legs.

My nose feels swollen and tight. A big sneeze builds and erupts as sudden as a musket shot. The horses jump and fret. Shadrach neighs in alarm. I blow my nose in my handkerchief again.

Then we don't move. We listen. Nothing.

I blow my nose once more — softly this time — and jam the handkerchief back up my sleeve. Mina rustles down through the hay and her hands re-emerge with a stoneware jug. With both hands, she hefts it over the rails to Eli. He sets it down on the floorboards with a thud. She passes another, and another, and another — four in all.

"How you know what's in them?" I whisper.

"Get the cork off," says Mina. "Take a whiff."

I take her word for it. "What are we going to do with it? Pour it out?"

"No!" Eli wails as loud as a whisper will allow. "Each take one."

"What about the fourth? Can you carry two, Eli?"

He shakes his head, then his eyes narrow and he frowns.

"We'll get *them*," he mutters.

We each lift a jug and follow him to the door. It weighs like an anvil. I set mine down while Eli returns for the fourth. He carries it past us into the sunlight.

"Eli! What are you doing?" I hiss. But he ignores me and marches toward the house. "Eli . . . "

"Shhh," whispers Mina. "Ain't no stopping him when he gets riled."

I can't believe he will do this — out there in the bright light, in full view of the windows. He reaches the foundation of the Dunwoody house. He leans against the brick wall while he pulls the cork out from the jug with his teeth. With both arms, he tilts the jug. Yellow contents spill onto the stone threshold of the kitchen door. *Glug-glug-glug.*

The stench hits me. This reek is no ordinary piss. It's been bottled up and fermented and pulls at my guts. It cuts through my stuffy nose like smelling salts.

Eli sprints around the garden and joins us. He drops the empty jug by the corner of the stable.

"That'll show 'em."

"Eli, you just gave them proof you did it before."

"Don't care. Let's go."

We each lug a full jug across the grass. By the time I reach the fence, the effects of the smell have worn off and my nose flows like liquid honey. I let the jug thud to the ground, and I reach up my sleeve for my handkerchief. Not there.

I pat my shirt, my trouser waist, my collar. No handkerchief anywhere. I blow my nose with my fingers. Mina is watching and I wish she wasn't.

Then I freeze.

"Get a move on, Slim."

My sleeve, my shirt, my trousers, my collar. Not there!

"I've got to go back."

"You crazy?"

"I've lost my handkerchief."

"Never mind. We gotta get outta here."

"It's one Mother gave me."

They look at each other across the fence. They understand. This is not about sentiment. It's evidence. Mother was proud of her needlework. In the evenings, she sat by the fire, squinting as she sewed monograms and patterns. Her butterflies and birds will link the handkerchief to me, as surely as the *JRG* in the corner of the linen.

"Hurry!"

I sprint back to the stable, alone. The empty jug lies by the doorway. From across the vegetable garden, the Dunwoodys' back door squeaks open. I slip into the darkness.

"Mary, what's that smell?" I don't hear a reply, but the man goes on, "Well, it sure . . . " And then he stops.

Through a knothole I watch Mr. Hawkins shade his eyes as he stares across the garden to where the empty jug lies. He strides toward the stable, his fists clenched. I drop to my knees and grope across the dark floor for the lost handkerchief. And my nose starts to itch again.

Mr. Hawkins's footsteps stop by the jug outside. Under his breath, he mutters words that Mother never let me use. I crouch by Belvedere's stall and wait for the door to open.

But the sounds fade away toward the fence. He is following our trail through the dew.

My eyes adjust to the dark and I can see the horses watching me. And there, down on the ground at the end of the stable, by the hay crib, white in the shadows, lies my handkerchief.

I can measure Mr. Hawkins's return from the string of bad words. I grab the handkerchief, slip over the rail of the crib, and bury myself in the hay. The seconds stretch long. The stable door opens. Surely he can hear my heart pounding.

And then my nose starts to itch again. I clutch my handkerchief in my right hand, and with it I squeeze the medicine bundle beneath my shirt. Squeeze it hard. The purple stone. The lion claw. I need the magic now. Save me. Make me invisible. Make my sound invisible. Spirit me away to anywhere but here.

My other hand pinches the bridge of my nose, hard. My eyes water and my nose runs like maple sap. I stem it with the handkerchief and breathe through my mouth, but it's only getting worse. Mr. Hawkins mumbles something to the horses.

I hear only a voice shouting in my head. Don't. Don't. Don't.

I do.

Of all the sneezes in all the world, this must be the loudest. The sneeze that rattles the stable rafters. The sneeze that sends horses prancing and squealing in their stalls. The sneeze that makes soldiers at the fort look up and turn toward town.

The sneeze that brings Mr. Hawkins to the hay crib. He reaches over the planks with his long, bony hand and grabs me by the ear.

He thrusts me forward. We burst into the sunlight and I sneeze and sneeze again. Then we hit the stench of fermented piss on the doorstep. My nose clears.

Inside the kitchen, he pushes me into a chair. Mrs. Hawkins waddles in from the lobby, tut-tuts, and disappears farther into the house. I dread a confrontation with Magistrate Dunwoody.

Slippers shuffle down the stairs in the lobby. The door swings open, but it's not William Dunwoody, Magistrate of Upper Canada. It's William Junior, still in his nightshirt, tying the sash of a silk nightgown. Even half-asleep, he struts like a prince. He wrinkles his nose and glances sourly at me.

"You?"

Behind him, fully dressed for the day, tromps Henry Ecker. He boards with the Dunwoody family, but obviously likes to rise earlier than William. He lifts his head, surprised. "I was expecting McCabe."

William watches me. "I'm so disappointed, Gibson. I thought we had an understanding the other day."

I don't reply.

"Stand up," he snaps. He slides into a seat at the other end of the table. I don't move. "Stand up!" he repeats. Henry walks over behind me and he and Mr. Hawkins lift me by my shirt. The chair clatters behind me.

They won't scare me. I slow my breathing and meet William's eyes.

"Where's Magistrate Dunwoody?"

"I'll ask the questions." William takes his eyes from mine for the first time. "Hawkins," he says, "fetch McKenney." He leans back in the chair. "Father has left for York. The house is in my charge."

From behind me, Henry chuckles. "Justice in your charge too?"

William smiles. "Justice by just us."

They don't say a word to me and the minutes stretch. At long last, a bell over the pantry door tinkles. Mrs. Hawkins's footsteps scurry across the lobby floor. Then comes the sound of other steps — Mr. Hawkins's shoes and the unmistakable *thump-stomp-thump-stomp* of Mr. McKenney on his wooden leg.

Good! Mr. McKenney will sort things out for me. But he stands at the doorway with his hat clutched in both hands, and he gives William a little bow.

William scowls. "The front door, McKenney?"

The jailor flushes. "I thought . . . given that this is official business and all . . . "

"It was my idea, young Master," Mr. Hawkins interjects. "No sense letting that smell in through the back door."

William glares at Mr. McKenney. "We have someone for you. The charge is public mischief."

"You've no right — " I blurt.

Henry's fist tightens on my collar. William cups his hands and studies his fingernails. "Young Gibson here will clean the smell off our threshold. Then you'll take him to your jail and you can keep him there until the next Quarter Session."

"But, begging your pardon, sir, don't you think . . . "

William looks up. "That's right, McKenney. *I* think. You obey."

The old man glances away.

The bell rings once more. Again Mrs. Hawkins's shoes *click-click-click* on the floor. "Magistrate Dunwoody is not at home," she scolds, "and young Master Dunwoody is busy right now."

There's no reply: just the sound of shoes marching briskly.

"I must ask you to leave!" Mrs. Hawkins's voice rises. "My husband will throw you out."

William calls, "Who is it, Mrs. Hawkins?"

The footsteps march straight toward the kitchen. The door opens. Eli's eyes shoot blue lightning.

"Let him go, Junior. He ain't done nothing."

William settles back in his chair, silent for a moment. He looks at Henry. "See? You let the constables come through the front door, and before long, all the riff-raff think it's their right."

"I knew it was McCabe's work," replies Henry. "This one's just the accomplice."

"Set the cheese and you'll catch the rat." William turns to Mr. McKenney. "Incarcerate both of them."

The little bell over the pantry tinkles again.

William looks at Henry. "This place is busier than the Yellow Tavern." He calls over his shoulder. "Mrs. Hawkins? No more visitors, if you please."

From the lobby, Mrs. Hawkins tells someone that Magistrate Dunwoody is not at home.

"Not a problem at all, Mrs. Hawkins." I know that breezy voice. "But I understand young William and Master Ecker are receiving guests and I thought I would drop by to pay my respects."

The footsteps do not hesitate. The door swings open. Mr. Willcocks takes one look around, and sniffs.

"Good morning, gentlemen. Best to get that mess cleaned up so we can open some windows, wouldn't you say?"

* * *

The nights are now almost as long as the days. We sit on the grass, throwing pebbles out into the black water. Ginger lies beside me, her head up, ears alert, enjoying the *plop*. Beyond the American fort, lightning illuminates the billowing clouds, followed by a rumble of thunder. But here the winds are calm, the lake still and the lighthouse beam arcs through the night.

"They was gonna send you to jail, Slim. I always reckoned it'd be my pa what would end up there. Not you."

Plop.

"So far, so good," I reply.

Plop.

"Reckon?"

I toy with the pebble in my fingers, listening to the crickets.

"It's like them there ripples," Eli continues. "My pa's in trouble for not showing up for militia. I'm in trouble on account of I'm his son. You're in trouble for being my friend. Now I suppose Mr. Willcocks has made enemies too."

A rumble of thunder makes Ginger turn her head. The wind picks up and stirs the trees behind us. Finally I throw my pebble far into the darkness. I hear it splash in the distance. We get up and hurry toward town.

"I think he was already in trouble with them."

"Well, he sure saved our bacon," Eli continues. "Do you think they woulda strung us up?"

"I beg your pardon?"

"My pa knowed someone what was taken out've a jail and strung up on the nearest oak tree."

"This is the Canadas, Eli. They have to give you a trial first."

He weighs that idea, nodding his head. "That's what Mr. Willcocks said, ain't it," he reflects, then turns to me. "You reckon we should ask him to join our brotherhood?"

Better to let Mina join the club. But I'd never suggest this. She was smart enough to fetch help from just the right person: not Father, not her pa, but Mr. Willcocks. I hope we can keep our morning's adventure a secret among us.

Huge raindrops splash in the dust. A flash of light-ning and, within seconds, the crack of thunder. The rain comes faster. I scramble over a fence and dash toward a shed. The rain pounds on the roof.

As we wait, I think back to the afternoon. Mr. Willcocks asked William what charges would be laid. Public mischief, William replied. But Mr. Willcocks cautioned him: lay those charges and there would be a trial. At a trial, questions would be raised about *earlier* episodes of public mischief. Did William and Henry really want a court to examine who sprayed the public buildings with urine? That was a month ago, but people still remember.

Then William replied that they would lock us up anyway and decide later. That's when Mr. Willcocks cleared his throat and lifted his head. I knew what that meant. I've heard him give speeches before. He can talk forever.

He began with a lesson on English history, but was just getting warmed up when he was interrupted by the sound of scrubbing. Mrs. Hawkins opened the door and there was Mina on her hands and knees with the brush and a bucket of soapy water, cleaning up the threshold. In the end, our only punishment was to help her finish the job.

A flash of lightning, but the sound comes from beyond the lighthouse. The storm is passing.

Eli turns to go, but then stops. "Thing about it is,

what's all that stuff about dead bodies?"

"What?"

"What Mr. Willcocks said."

"He didn't say anything about dead bodies."

"Plain as plain, Slim." He lowers his voice to a loud whisper. "They was going to hang up those dead bodies — rotting and stinking."

"Eli, no one said a thing about dead bodies."

"The *corpses*," he says. "He was going to hang the hideous corpses."

I start to giggle. I try to keep it quiet, but I can't. "Eli," I gasp between breaths, "he wasn't talking about hanging dead bodies. He said 'suspend *habeas corpus*.' It means putting you in jail without telling you why."

"Then why didn't he *say* so?"

"It's a Latin term. Dominie Burns told us about it."

He shrugs and turns away. "Corn! I don't know why folks are forever talking in Latin. It doesn't seem right. Not here, nohow."

"Good night," I call after him.

"Good night."

His footsteps splash into the darkness.

THE UPPER CANADA GUARDIAN

September–December 1811

"Jacob?"

"Yes, Father."

"Come in here please."

Uh-oh. He's waiting in the parlour. Not a good sign. And Mr. Willcocks is with him, his top hat on the table, and his hands folded over the brass knob of his walking stick. Has he told Father about our urine war with William and Henry?

The parlour is for entertaining guests, for funerals, and for only the most important discussions. I must be in even more trouble than I thought. I try to read Mr. Willcocks's face. Grave. No hint of his good-natured twinkle.

"Have a seat," Father says.

The chair. When he upbraids me, Father usually makes me stand. This is deeper trouble than I've ever known.

They sit at opposite ends of the settee, upright and serious. I take a place in the wooden chair, my back as stiff and straight as Mr. Willcocks's walking stick.

"Mr. Willcocks has been observing you these past months," Father continues. I wait. "He's impressed with your abilities and your intelligence. He thinks you have potential."

"Thank you," I mumble. Whenever adults talk like this, the next sentence usually begins with, "But . . . "

"And," Father says, "he wants to know if you will become his apprentice."

"I beg your pardon?"

I glance back and forth between them — so formal and serious. Then Mr. Willcocks breaks into a smile.

"Come to the *Upper Canada Guardian*, young man. Tom Kelly will show you how to set type and, before long, you'll be big enough to help Stephenson pull The Beast's tail."

"You want me to work for you?"

"Don't make it sound like a death sentence, lad!"

"Sorry."

"Sorry for looking like you're mounting the scaffold?" Mr. Willcocks continues. "Or sorry for turning me down?"

"It's just that . . . "

"You know, Robert, he's usually not so tongue-tied."

"This will be in addition to your current responsibilities, Jacob." Father's face is set. "And I still expect you to tend to the chickens and milk Dolley. You'll help me in the store when you can."

"And you'll maintain your studies, of course," adds Mr. Willcocks. "But we'll teach you a few things you won't find in the dominie's classroom."

The *Upper Canada Guardian*! I'll be right at the centre of the action. Not just in our own town, but the entire province. The news from around the whole world comes to the *Guardian* before anyone else knows it.

"I believe Mr. Willcocks is waiting for an answer, Jacob."

I grin my reply.

* * *

"I reckon this is better'n stirring a tannery vat."

"Just as messy," I reply, "but not as smelly."

"Depends," Eli says. "Can't smell the vat. But *that* stuff sure stinks."

The newspaper office takes up two rooms in Mr. Willcocks's house. In the front room, we sit cross-legged on the floorboards beside The Beast. That's the name Mr. Stephenson gives to the printing press standing in the middle. Ginger dozes in the corner.

We mix soot with a mixture of water, walnut oil and oil of turpentine. Our hands, faces and clothes are smudged with black. We're making ink. My other job is to return the letters to the type case in the back room once the page has been printed. This is much harder than I thought it would be. "Mind your Ps and Qs," Mr. Kelly often scolds.

I've heard that expression many times. Now I think it should be: "Mind your Ps and Qs, and your Bs and Ds."

Mr. Kelly has worked so long as a typesetter that his hands fly back and forth from the type case to the galley as he takes dictation from Mr. Willcocks. It's easy to get lower-case letters mixed up, but if I put a *p, q, b* or *d* in the wrong box, it slows him right down and he gets mad.

The pages of the upcoming issue have been printed. Mr. Stephenson and Mr. Kelly have gone to the Yellow Tavern with Mr. Willcocks.

My job isn't done until I've replenished the ink supply. I probably should have asked permission to bring Eli in to help me.

Smudges of soot cover our hands and faces. We might as well be apprenticed as chimney sweeps.

"Sounds like Old Buzzardnose sure beat at your rug the other day," Eli says.

That's Eli's nickname for the dominie. And he is right. When word spread that I was apprenticing at the *Guardian*, Dominie Burns made me stand before the whole class. "You will be Daniel in the lions' den," he said. I replied, "Yes, sir," but I didn't really understand why.

Then Dominie Burns continued, "There are those who would bring us down. Level us. Turn us into," and he paused and sneered the words, "*a democracy.* Look at France. Look at those so-called United States of America." He wrinkled his big nose in distaste.

I didn't know how to respond to that. Maybe he didn't expect a reply.

"Yes, sir," I repeated, and resumed my seat.

The blackboard squeaked with chalk as the dominie wrote:

GOD

KING

EMPIRE

He turned to face us, his feet apart and his hands clasped behind his back — a captain on a quarterdeck. Then he returned to the blackboard and slashed an X across *KING.* "When you remove the King, you undermine natural order." He stood silent, waiting for his words to sink in. "Some would poison our minds with democratic ideas," he continued. "These men are quick with words. They know how to raise the rabble and the mob." Then Dominie Burns stared at me. "And some of them," he said, "publish *newspapers.*"

"Yep, he beat at your rug," Eli repeated, "and left you hanging on the line. I thought you was the dominie's favourite."

I stir the ink. "It wasn't as bad as all that," I say at last. But Eli is right: it certainly feels strange to have

Dominie Burns single me out like that. I've been his star scholar. "I guess Dominie Burns doesn't like this newspaper."

Eli shrugs. "Just this one? Or all of 'em?"

I hadn't thought of that. The *Guardian* isn't the only newspaper in Upper Canada — just the most popular one. "He wants it to be like it was before," I say. "The Governor once fired a newspaper publisher."

"Really?"

"Before I was born."

"They can't do that to Mr. Willcocks — can they?"

"In France" — I lean forward; this is getting exciting — "they cut off their *heads*. With a guillotine." I motion with my hand the blade descending.

Eli nods. "What they do in England? Hang 'em?"

"They used to smash up the printing presses. But not now. Mr. Willcocks says there's *rule of law and a free press*." I say the words the way Mr. Willcocks does — like it's something holy.

"Better'n being hanged, I reckon." Eli scratches his scalp, but the soot is lost among all that black hair. "Slim?"

I look up.

"You're learning a lot working for this here newspaper."

I shrug. Mr. Willcocks talks a lot. Around here, you can't help but learn.

"I was thinking . . . "

"What, Eli?"

"When you get too smart for me . . . are we still gonna be friends?"

I grin at him. "You're my blood brother."

He nods and returns to the mixture. "Just want to make sure," he says to the ink. "Sometimes people grow up and drift apart."

"Never. Not us."

I add a little more turpentine to the mix and keep stirring. Eli looks up at me. "You're painted up like an Injun."

I wipe my cheek. I've probably only made my face dirtier. "You too."

"You figure this is what they use for war paint?"

I dip my finger in the ink mixture and spread it across my cheekbone, then look for Eli's reaction. He reaches over and takes a little ink to draw a line down his nose. Ginger rises from the corner and pads over, tail wagging.

"Them Injuns paint their dogs too?"

"Careful. Don't spill."

"I'm Shenandoah. Pa says he fought for Liberty."

"Oh yeah? Well, I'm Joseph Brant. He fought for the King."

"Can't be much of a Injun with a name like that. Shenandoah's better."

"Oh yeah? We were better fighters."

"Says who?"

"Me, that's who."

"I'm gonna scalp you."

"No, I'm going to scalp *you*!"

I grab at Eli's hair and he tries to grab mine. We scuffle and push toward the doorway. In the close quarters of the back room, his size is less of an advantage to him. If I can go for his knees, I can drop him.

I heave with all my strength and down we go. We slam hard into the typesetting case.

"Stop!" I yell.

We let go of each other and I leap up to steady the type case. It's divided into small boxes and each box is full of lead and wooden letters. None of those letters weighs more than a grasshopper, but put them all together on that big, towering case, and they're as heavy as a giant oak tree. Just as immovable too — that's what I thought.

But now the case teeters, the letters move, the weight shifts.

We scramble out of the way. Ginger scampers to the press room with a yelp, tail between her legs. With a crash, the letters scatter everywhere on the planks.

We stand there. Ginger pokes her head through the doorway, looks at the mess, looks at us, retreats. We lift the case back onto the table.

"How we gonna put them all back?"

"Mind your Ps and Qs," I say. "And Bs and Ds."

* * *

By suppertime we've made little progress cleaning up the type. We'll have to do it later tonight, to keep anyone from finding out.

After Father thinks I'm in bed, I sneak out. Ginger frets behind the door, but does not bark or whine. The streets are quiet under a dusting of snow and the stars shine brightly. I unlock the newspaper office, and light a candle in the lantern. Eli arrives.

"Who'd think you'd need so many of these little fellers to print a newspaper," he says. With the lantern on the floor, our shadows stretch up the walls and across the ceiling. "Is this a p or a q?"

"Leave all the tricky ones. I'll do them later."

I had scrubbed my hands before dinner, but picking up thousands of letters blackens them again. Eli's cheeks and nose are soon smeared with ink.

"Eli, no one must ever know this happened."

He nods.

"They can't know you were here either."

"Right."

"I'd be dismissed for sure."

"You reckon we'll be done by daybreak?"

Then from the next room, a rattle on the door.

We both freeze. There it is again, then the sound of metal on metal — the faint click of a door latch.

Voices.

"It's unlocked?" asks one softly.

"Trusting soul." I know those voices. William and Henry.

"Foolish, I'd say."

I blow out the lamp and darkness swallows our room. Then light flows through the doorway.

"Start with the press?" says Henry's voice.

"The type first."

Footsteps approach. The shaft of light grows brighter. A hand holding a lantern stretches through the doorway. Then William enters. In his other hand, he holds a crowbar.

"What are you doing here?" I wish my voice was deep and angry, but it cracks and squeaks.

William shouts. He jumps back and almost drops the lantern.

I stride after him into the printing-press room. Eli stays behind in the shadows. Good idea. He's not supposed to be here.

"What are *you two* doing here?" I repeat.

"Gibson!" pants William. "It's only you."

"What are you *doing* here?" And then it dawns on me. "You've come to damage the printing press!"

William surveys me and says nothing. He puts the crowbar down on the printing press.

"War is coming, Gibson," says Henry. He's carrying an axe. He's trying to hide it behind his back. "It's time to prepare."

"It's time," William smirks at Henry, and turns back to me, "to purify this community."

I try to control my voice. "Purify?"

William's voice is calm. "We're going to rid Upper Canada of anyone whose loyalty is suspect."

"Is this Dominie Burns's idea?"

Henry says, "We don't need anyone to tell us what needs to be done."

I turn to William. "You're the magistrate's son."

"My father knows nothing of this."

"I'll tell him."

"You have no witnesses, Gibson. Just your word against the two of us."

From the shadows in the next room, a voice calls out, "Well now, Junior, that ain't exactly right." Eli steps from the darkness.

"Turd Boy! You're even worse than Willcocks. We're not finished with you yet."

"I reckon you're finished for tonight," Eli drawls. He wipes his nose with his sleeve and the ink smears across his cheek. "Purify," he scoffs. "Reckon in this world, everyone's gotta live with a little dirt — even you two."

They don't turn their backs to us as they slip out the door.

ARSON

December 1811–February 1812

"Father?"

"Pay attention, Jacob, or you'll lose a thumb."

I pull my hands away. He swings the axe and splits the log in two. Each half flies sideways and lands in the rubble. I pick up one of the halves and place it upright in the centre of the big stump.

"Can't we tell them we don't want a war?"

"Tell whom?"

The axe swings down. Two quarter logs jump. I pick out the other half and lay it on the stump.

"I don't know. The King? General Brock?"

"It's not up to them."

"Then who?" I correct myself: "*Whom?*"

Crack. I set up another whole log.

"The President," he grunts as he swings, "of the United States."

This time, the blade is stuck. Father pounds it up and down until the log tears apart.

"Tell *him* then."

He rests his boot on the stump and looks at me.

"I'll do that" — he wipes the sweat from his forehead — "the next time I see him."

A cold wind blows up from the lake through the bare branches of the orchards, but he has unbuttoned his shirt.

"If there is a war, do we have to purify the town?"

"Purify?"

"You know, make it clean. Get rid of anyone who won't defend the King?"

He looks at me in surprise. "Joe Willcocks didn't say that, did he?"

"No." I search for an explanation. "I heard it at school."

"Dominie Burns?" Father looks annoyed.

"From some of the other boys."

"Without due process? What kind of despot would do that?" he says, and he takes a mighty swing that sends the wood flying. "We're at war with France because we're protecting our freedom from despots."

"What's a despot?"

"Someone who has authority, and no one to stop him." Father sits down on the stump and rotates one arm, then the other. Some day soon I'll be old enough to help him with the splitting.

"Like Napoleon?"

"That's right."

"And General Brock?"

"What?"

"Mr. Willcocks says that it's a bad idea — having one man in charge of the army *and* the government too."

Father kneels on the ground and picks up split wood. I join him. "It's different," he says. "General Brock is only in charge of the government temporarily. The Governor will return from England some day. And the General still answers to King George." He has overloaded his arm with wood, and one piece tumbles back to the ground. "And most of all," he says as he retrieves the stick, "the General is an honourable man."

"But what if people do bad things in his name?"

He pauses. "What kind of bad things?"

I'm treading on dangerous ground here. No one must know that Eli and I spilled the type case. I kneel down and pick up wood.

"Oh, I don't know. Something . . . like . . . smash a printing press, maybe?"

He's looking at me, I can tell.

"Is there something you're not telling me, Jacob?"

I need to change the topic, fast.

"Mr. Willcocks says that used to happen in England — when the government got mad at the newspaper." I rise to my feet with my armload of split logs and follow him toward the house.

"The important thing — " he begins to stack the

wood by the back door — " is that we protect our liberties as British subjects." He heaves the last piece to the top of the stack. I follow him back to the woodpile.

"The rule of law?" I ask him. "A free press?"

"Now that sounds more like Joe Willcocks," he says and picks up the axe. He looks at me a moment, then offers the handle to me. "Here. You want to try?"

* * *

As night falls, Eli scrapes cowhide by lantern light. We're in the mill, and the river gurgles below us. "If you were up to your neck in the tannery vat," he says, "and someone threw a bucket of puke . . . " He turns to face me. "Would you duck?"

I laugh. "That's what they call a dilemma."

Ginger lifts her head from my lap, rises to her paws, and stretches.

"Here's another one for you," he says. "If you could make lots of money tanning leather, would you want to stay Turd Boy?"

"Don't let them get to you, Eli."

"Some day I'll take over Pa's tannery. But there's got to be other ways to make a living here."

"Some day I'll run a newspaper and you could work with me. You could pull The Beast's tail."

"Too boring," he says. "And not enough money, I reckon. But take this mill." He gestures with his knife at the grindstones. "We could use it for more than crushing wood."

"Sure."

"We could build a sawmill too."

"That's a good idea, Eli. People are building houses all the time."

"I'd like that — building houses."

We stop and watch Ginger. She's whining and whimpering at the door. Then she barks.

"I always wanted to be a soldier," I say. "A real one. Like at the fort. But Mother wanted me to be a teacher."

"Like Old Buzzardnose?" Eli laughs. "Corn, Slim, I can't picture you wearing one of those gowns and a silly hat."

"Ginger, enough!"

She won't stop barking at the door. She runs up a few steps, then back down to the door, snapping and barking at the latch. I pull myself to my feet. "You smell something?"

No use asking Eli.

But he says, "Smoke . . . "

I clatter down the stairs and swing the door open and Ginger dashes outside.

"Fire!" I shout up the hill. "*Fire!*"

Flames are licking the sides of the vat shed. They light up the darkness.

"*Fire!*" Eli yells.

Ginger sprints ahead and disappears into the trees up the hill.

The flames are like snakes slithering up the dried boards. I toss handfuls of snow onto them. They hiss and spit back steam.

Eli throws another armload of snow. "Pa! Ma! *Fire!*"

What if someone's inside? I rush to the entrance and swing the door wide. A burst of flame staggers me.

No one inside. The fire spreads across the plank floor.

The McCabe family rushes down from the house, Mina hustling the younger children as Mr. and Mrs. McCabe run ahead. He carries a bucket in each fist and tosses one to Eli.

Farther up the road, Mr. McKenney hobbles toward us on his wooden leg. And now there's Father, carrying an axe. And others with crowbars and buckets. Soldiers. They carry beer tankards from the taverns.

A big lieutenant shouts, "I want a bucket line. You there —" he grabs Mr. McCabe. "You're the marker. Everyone behind him."

I run with Father down to the lake. His axe smashes through an ice-fishing hole. He lowers a bucket and lifts it to me. I need both hands to pass it to the soldier beside me. The water slops over the rim and stings my fingers.

Father fills a second bucket and I stagger with the weight. My arms are not going to take much of this.

The lieutenant shouts out commands. "Two lines. Women and children to the left. Men to the right."

Mina passes me an empty bucket. I pass it to my father, who fills it in the lake, and heaves it up to a soldier. Hundreds of people have lined up between the hole in the ice and the blazing shed. We move faster, faster, a machine, but the flames grow brighter.

Up and down the line, all the dogs of the town bark and play. Ginger is having a wonderful time.

Then the buckets stop coming. The flames leap high into the night. We've lost.

Father takes my hand in his. It's cold as ice. We follow the crowd toward the blaze.

Mina sobs into her father's shoulder and he glares at the flames. Mrs. McCabe stands beside him, watching his face.

Mr. McKenney has collapsed into the snow. Mr. Willcocks offers him a flask. "Take care that leg of yours doesn't catch fire," he says, but the laughter is empty. Mr. Dunwoody asks the big lieutenant what he knows about the fire's cause.

I press close to Father. I don't think my hands will ever be warm again, in spite of the heat from the bonfire. Ginger sits on her haunches, her eyes bright.

The walls of the shed have burned away, and the rafters and roof flame brightly. They sag, sag some more, then collapse with an explosion of sparks. Burning timbers splash into the vat. The stench rises with the steam.

A soldier says to another, "What say you? Will it burn?"

The other shakes his head. "Liquid will keep it from catching fire."

"A dollar says it burns." Within a few minutes, he's taking bets from all sides.

The flames lick at the bottom of the slats. The steam rises faster.

"I think you're going to lose your bet," says Mr. Willcocks and the lieutenant shouts, "Clear out of there! It's going to blow!" On the downward slope, the crowd scatters.

With a boom and a whoosh, the vat's contents burst through the slats. The liquid pours over the flames with a hiss and oozes downhill toward the lake. Ginger rises from her haunches and trots over to the soggy snow. She squats and adds her own bit.

* * *

The stench of smoke hovers in the morning air as I milk Dolley, feed Solomon and Excalibur, and collect the eggs from the henhouse. Then I head over to Eli's. It's morning, but the skies grow darker. Snow is coming.

Below King Street, a sheet of brownish-yellow

ice, as smooth as a serving tray, has spread from the shoreline. Ginger runs on ahead and sits at Eli's feet among the smouldering rubble. He stares across the lake.

"I been thinking." He scrapes a stick over the ashes. "There's got to be some use for all that there frozen pee."

"I'm not going skating on it, if that's what you're thinking."

"All that waste. Maybe we can cut out big blocks of it. Wonder what the tanners in York would pay?"

"Just don't sell it next summer as lemonade with crushed ice."

He laughs and looks at me. "Ship it to them rich fellers in New York City or Montreal."

"What's your pa going to do now?"

"It'll take a long time to replace that."

"Maybe there's more in the Dunwoody stable." I mean this as a joke, but his smile dies.

"Slim" — he turns to me — "where were they?"

"Who?"

"Junior. Lug. I didn't see hide nor hair of 'em last night."

"Everyone was here, Eli. I think . . ."

"Yeah." He nods. "The whole durned town. But not Junior."

"And not Henry."

He rises to his feet. "Let's do us some tracking."

I follow him up the slope toward the trees. The first snowflakes begin to fall, big and wet from a south-west wind.

"You'll never find tracks," I call. "There were hundreds of people."

"Yup. Stomped the snow flatter'n the market square."

We cut along the path to the burying ground where the snow is fresh. "Hey, Slim! Here's Ginger's tracks. And she's running."

Off to the other side, I see a pair of boot tracks — toes mostly — spread far apart. "Here's someone. Running too."

"And over here! Someone else. Big boots."

We follow the tracks. Little Boots and Big Boots were sprinting. Up into the burying ground and past the gravestones.

And here, near the church, they stop and turn. They jumble together with dog prints. Blood! Small drops of it in the snow.

Eli bends on one knee to study the drops. "Ginger caught up with them," he says.

"Good girl!"

But Ginger sniffs around the gravestones, unconcerned.

"Here!" I shout. "Here's a stick. With bite marks in it. Big Boots used it to fight Ginger while Little Boots kept running."

The tracks tell the story. Big Boots made a stand. Ginger circled around. And the tracks of Little Boots lead to . . .

"Hoofprints," says Eli.

Yes, two sets of horse tracks coming from the church. Big Boots backs toward them, turns, and then there are no boot tracks at all — only horse tracks galloping toward the road, with dog tracks in pursuit.

I look up at the church spire and watch the flakes. The snow is falling faster now, covering the tops of the tombstones as we head back to the tannery. It lands on the bloody snow, and on the tracks of horses, dog and boots.

Did someone set fire to the vat shed? If so, then who? We have nothing that will stand in a court of law — nothing at all once the snow buries the evidence.

But we have our suspicions.

Eli looks across the white landscape. "I reckon the tannery's done been purified."

* * *

You see the world differently when you climb a tree. Higher than everyone, you see more and maybe you know more. Is this why adults tell us what to do? They see more from their height? Is this what Magistrate Dunwoody feels like when he sits on his bench at the courthouse?

No adults here. And we're the prosecution, the judge and jury.

"How long you reckon we got to wait?" asks Eli.

I don't have an answer, so I don't reply. I shift my position where I crouch on a bough. I watch Ginger where she noses about at the riverbank.

"We shoulda brought a rope," Eli continues.

I look down at Eli. "We're not going to hang them. We'll take them to court."

"If we had a rope, you could swing down and knock them outta their saddles."

I think about this. "And if we had a rope," I add, "we could tie them up once we've captured them."

"Maybe we should go get one."

I don't reply, but I know there's no time. We don't know when they're coming, but sooner or later, William and Henry will ride down this road. They left for Queenston the night of the fire, and today they return to Newark.

How do we know? Mina says so. How does she know? She will not say.

"What does she see in those two?"

"Who?"

"Your sister."

"What's that got to do with rope?" He looks up quizzically. "Are you sweet on my sister?"

"No!"

"Careful, Slim. You're gonna fall outta that tree."

I squint down the road. "Eli, someone's coming. Hide!"

Eli slips behind the tree trunk. I flatten onto the bough. A carriage rattles over the frozen ruts. This won't be William and Henry — not in a carriage — but we can test our hiding places.

Ginger has other ideas. She loves this game. When she cannot see us, she trots up from the river. She barks and sniffs eagerly around the trunk. As the carriage draws close, she looks up and barks in triumph. The carriage rolls to a halt below me.

"Master Gibson!" calls a voice I know too well. "What are you doing up in that tree?"

"Studying botany, sir."

Dominie Burns rises in the carriage, and the springs squeak. He adjusts his spectacles. "Botany?"

"Yes, sir. What happens to tree moss in the winter?"

"There is tree moss up there?"

"No, sir. I guess that's what happens."

"Do you need help down?"

I shake my head.

"Well, good day to you then."

He snaps the reins and the carriage rolls on. Eli emerges from behind the tree.

"Maybe we shouldn't have brought Ginger after all," I say.

"Can't do nothing about that now."

"Hide!"

Eli grabs Ginger and flattens behind the tree trunk. I lie low on the bough. Up the road, two riders trot side by side. On Meshach's back, William posts like he and the horse move with one mind. On Abednego, Henry nurses a bandaged hand.

They move fast. I slip my hand under my coat and squeeze the medicine bundle for good luck. Time it right, or . . .

A sharp yelp from behind the trunk. Ginger wriggles loose from Eli's arms and stands in the middle of the road, snarling and baring her teeth.

They halt ten yards up the road. William looks up. "Gibson! Call off your dog."

Henry won't take his eyes off Ginger. Spittle sprays from her mouth as she barks.

I say as calmly as I can, "She sure seems to hate Henry."

William glares at me. "We shoot dogs that bite people."

Eli slips out from behind the tree and stands beside Ginger in the roadway. "Looks like you already been bit, Lug." He nods at Henry's bandaged hand. "Now, I wonder how that happened."

"We know Ginger bit you!" I wish I could keep my voice as calm as Eli's. "At the burying ground."

"We know it was you what torched my pa's shed," adds Eli. "You're gonna fess up."

"You think so?" replies William. "How quaint."

He spurs Meshach and lunges forward. Henry grabs his pommel in pursuit.

Ready . . . ready . . .

Now!

I aim for the dark shape hurtling below me.

Meshach neighs and it sounds like a scream as he jumps aside on all four legs.

I thud against his flank. William topples over into the snow.

Henry and Abednego lurch past, pounding Eli back onto the ground. Meshach follows, the empty stirrups flying.

For a moment, three of us lie there on the ground, stunned. William rises to his hands and knees. I lift myself to my elbows. Eli rolls over and shakes his head.

In the distance, Ginger's barking is getting louder. Closer.

William rises to his feet. Two horses thunder toward me, followed by a defiant dog. I roll aside as the hooves stamp around me.

The horses turn, and here's Henry on Abednego, offering Meshach's reins to William. William grips the pommel and leaps onto Meshach's saddle. Ginger chases them in full battle cry.

Eli and I pick ourselves up and watch them disappear down the road.

"Corn, Slim." Eli shakes his head. "Them two ain't for the flank companies. Them's cavalry!"

GINGER

February 1812

"Father?"

"Yes, Jacob."

"Can I get a horse?"

"You've got Solomon."

"He's not my horse. And he's so big. And you won't let me ride Excalibur. I need a horse of my own."

In the gathering dusk, I'm cleaning Solomon's hooves. You have to be gentle but strong. Lean and push against Solomon's side so he will lift his leg and I can draw up his hoof. Father thinks I'm strong enough now.

"The Dunwoodys have three horses, just for riding. *And* a carriage horse like Solomon."

I look back over my shoulder. Father concentrates on brushing Excalibur's tail. One day I'll be able to ride Excalibur, but he is very excitable.

"The Dunwoodys hire people to take care of four horses."

"I could take care of three. Promise!"

"You've got a lot on your plate right now, son. School. The chores. The newspaper." He raises his eyes to meet mine. "And you're spending a lot of time at the McCabes'." He concentrates on Excalibur's tail again. "We'll help them rebuild their vat shed."

I still have no proof that William and Henry set the fire.

"Do you think the fire was an accident?" I ask.

"That's what they say."

From beyond the stable, Cathleen calls, "Mr. Gibson?" Her voice is urgent.

The door swings open and Ginger awakens from where she has been napping in the straw.

"Mr. Gibson, that man is here to see you."

"What man?"

"Mr. McKenney. From the jailhouse. And he's carrying a musket. He says it's important."

Father puts the brush down and heads for the door. Ginger rises to follow him, but I have a bad feeling.

"Ginger, stay." I latch the door behind me and she whines in complaint.

My gut tells me this is not good. Not good at all.

They stand in the doorway.

"You will do no such thing," Father growls. "You have no right!"

Mr. McKenney sounds like there are many other places he would rather be. His words are slurred.

"The orders come from Magistrate Dunwoody."

"Since when does Mr. Dunwoody's authority extend to animals, Mr. McKenney?"

"I don't know, sir. I just do what he tells me. He says your dog bit someone. I've been told to shoot the dog."

I sprint back to the stable.

"C'mon, girl. We have to hide."

Night is falling. Their voices follow me across the snow.

"I can take him to the dump. Where no one will see."

"You'll do no such thing."

Now it's Mr. McKenney whose voice is angry. "Or I'll shoot him in the street the next time I see him. I have a warrant right here, Mr. Gibson. It's from the magistrate himself."

No one sees Ginger and me as we run up the rise and down to the lakeshore. The beach is deserted. Where can we go? Ginger trots on ahead toward the McCabes'.

This is evil genius. Henry's injured hand links him to the scene of the crime, where Ginger bit him. But now Henry says Ginger bit him on the road from Queenston.

A lie. A terrible lie. And I could prove it a lie at a trial. Henry's story would not stand up in court. But there's no justice for dogs. Just Mr. McKenney and his musket.

Candlelight glows from the McCabe house. Do I knock?

Sooner or later, Mr. McKenney will come looking for Ginger at the McCabes'. I don't want Jed or Benjamin blurting out that they've seen us. And Mina? She's been telling Eli and me about those two. What's she telling them about *us*? The only one I can trust is my blood brother. I turn from the house and push the door to the mill by the water.

"Eli? You here?"

A short, startled cry.

"Gosh, Jake. You nearly scared me outta my shoes. What you doing skulking about?"

A lantern rests on the top step. Mina stands there, holding a broom.

"Don't let the draught in. Close the door," she says. Then she spots Ginger. "Hello, girl."

Ginger's tail thumps against the railing as she climbs. From the bottom of the stairs, I can see more of Mina's leg than I should.

"You gonna stand there all night? It's warmer up here."

"I . . . I came to see Eli . . . "

"He's fixing to have supper. Pa's in a mood and it's best I stay out of sight." She sits on the stairs. "So, if you're hungry, you can have mine."

I climb the steps. Mina smells of soap. Such a sweet smell.

"Do . . . do you think there's something they can give Ginger?"

"Reckon that's no problem." She looks at me intently. "What's wrong, Jake?"

I hesitate. "They want to kill Ginger." I glance into the shadows, then find her eyes again. "Mr. McKenney has a musket." I hold back tears. "They say she bit Henry. She did, but not like they say, and it's Henry who should be shot, and William, because they set the fire. But now they want to kill Ginger."

"Hey . . . Hey, slow down." She sits me down beside her.

I take a few deep breaths. Then I talk more calmly. When I've finished, she shakes her head. "You and my little brother. Jumping outta trees!"

"Someone's got to stop them."

She shrugs. "William's nice to me."

"You actually *like* him?"

"Jake, a girl's gotta find friends where she can."

"Him?"

"He ain't no Prince Charming maybe, but he does know how to make a girl feel special."

"But not . . . *him!*"

"Jake, sooner or later I'm gonna have to leave Ma and Pa. That's the way of the world."

"He's not going to marry you."

"No. That's a fact."

"Then why?"

"He knows people what can help."

"He's not *helping* you, Mina. He burned down your father's shed. He tried to put Eli and me in jail. He wants to kill Ginger."

"Jake, I gotta make my own way in the world — sooner or later. I got a better chance with friends like him."

"Mina, you're too good for him."

She brushes her hand across my cheek. "Aw, Jakie, that's so sweet."

I don't want to be sweet. I don't want any sympathy. I want to save Ginger.

"He's not going to get my dog. We're going to run away."

"Where?"

I hesitate. Can I trust her? But I'm desperate for help. "I don't know. The woods. Queenston. The Indian country. Anywhere."

"Maybe you could hide Ginger here?" Mina says. "For a while, anyways."

She looks so kind, so caring. Is it possible she would betray us?

"You won't . . . tell . . . *them?*"

She shakes her head. "I ain't gonna tell no one. Not even my little brother."

"But Eli's got to know . . . "

She takes my hand. "Jake, best Eli don't know nothing."

Beyond the walls, out on the street, someone pounds on the door to the McCabe house. Mina rises from the step and moves silently to the mill entrance.

"Keep quiet," she whispers.

I crouch beside Mina by the door, holding Ginger tight. Her hackles rise. A growl rumbles deep in her throat.

"Shhh, girl." She looks at me. In the street, men argue in the lantern light. Mr. McCabe is a big man and he stands his ground, his voice rising.

"You say you got yourself a warrant for a dog. I ain't got no dog. And I bet there ain't nothing in your paper says you can disturb a man's dinner."

Eli's silhouette leans forward.

"I ain't seen Jake, and I ain't seen Ginger, and they ain't here."

Mr. McKenney is easy to identify with his wooden leg and the musket. Behind him at a distance, William and Henry stand beside Mr. Hawkins, who holds the lantern.

William steps forward. He speaks in a voice so low I can't hear.

"Get out!" Mr. McCabe snaps.

"I know how you got that there dog bite," shouts Eli, "and t'weren't on no road from Queenston."

Nobody moves. William raises his voice. "We'll be back."

Mina looks at me. "You two can't stay here. Any other place to hide Ginger?"

I can think of only one.

* * *

These days, the afternoon sun melts the snow, but at this early hour, the dead grass lies stiff with frost. I stand by the bridge at Four Mile Creek. Below, the black water gurgles beneath the gaps in the ice.

A man in an overcoat hauls a carpet bag across the bridge. I was hoping to be alone. I have walked all this way so that we won't be disturbed when we say goodbye to each other.

"Waiting for the coach?" he asks.

I nod. He dumps his bag beside me and unbuttons his overcoat. He pulls a timepiece out of his waistcoat pocket and studies it.

"Shouldn't be long now," he says, then turns back to me. "You're Rob Gibson's boy, ain't ya? Long way from home, son."

Four miles, to be exact. A lonely distance without either Eli or Ginger.

"So, where you off to? Forty Mile? Ancaster?"

I look out toward the lake. "I'm meeting someone."

He frowns. "Long way to come. At this hour." I don't reply. "Cat's got your tongue?" His breath leaves puffs in the chilly air.

From beyond the trees, the rattle of wheels and the

jingle of harness. A carriage with four horses rounds the corner. The driver hauls back on the reins.

As the coach pulls up, the door thumps and bumps. Even before the wheels roll to a stop, the door swings open. A sharp, joyful bark that I know so well. Ginger tumbles out of the coach, races across the road and bowls me over.

"Dog's got your tongue, I reckon," says the man. He calls over to the coach, "That you, Joe Willcocks? You my travelling companion today?"

Ginger and I roll in the snow and the frozen mud. She licks my face and breaks off to scamper around in circles.

I glance back and catch Mr. Willcocks's laughing eyes as he turns to the traveller. "I'm your companion, Willie, and so is this fine dog." He climbs down and shakes the man's hand.

"The dog gonna vote in the Assembly too?"

Mr. Willcocks chuckles. "I'll take votes wherever I can get them."

"You hang in there, Joe. We're with ya."

The two men wander off.

Ginger races three times around the frozen mud in a circle. I chase after, and she yelps and scampers across the bridge, then back to me.

The driver takes the carpet bag and tosses it into the carriage. Only a few minutes left.

Mr. Willcocks walks over to us.

"You sure you want to do this?"

I nod my head. I scratch under Ginger's fur along her back, all the way to her ears. Her eyes shine like a puppy's.

"It could be a long time," he continues.

I rise to my feet. Ginger takes this as an invitation to play and begins to run her circles again.

"I'll write," I tell Mr. Willcocks.

He nods and shakes my hand, and we return to the door of the coach.

The driver lumbers over to Mr. Willcocks. "This wasn't part of the deal, Joe. That dog was nice and quiet when we left."

"She'll be fine."

"Is the lad coming too? You paid for the dog but not the lad."

"He stays here."

The driver harrumphs. The man with the over-coat sits inside the coach and studies his watch again. "We leaving on time, Angus? Or should I go back home for more breakfast?"

"Just get Joe's dang-burned dog inside, and we're off."

I want to shout: *She's not a dang-burned dog; her name is Ginger; and she's not Mr. Willcocks's dog; she's mine!* But I don't know if that's true anymore.

One thing's for sure: Ginger doesn't want to stop playing.

"Get inside," Mr. Willcocks whispers to me. "She'll follow."

The springs creak as I haul myself up the step. The interior is stuffed with baggage, and smells of pipe smoke. Ginger's hind paws scramble and scrape on the steps as she leaps after me. Her tail thumps against the man's leg.

"Hope she settles down," he says doubtfully.

"She'll be fine," says Mr. Willcocks as he closes the door behind him. "Now, Jacob. You ready?"

I'm not ready. I'll never be ready. Not for this. But I rise from my seat and slip past Mr. Willcocks's long legs and open the door just enough to let me through.

Ginger barks, as if she's thinking this is another game. Then I take the handle in both hands and shut the door quickly, but not fast enough. The door catches her head and she yelps and retreats. The latch clicks. She barks again. A different tone this time.

"Hope she ain't gonna make a racket all the way to York," grumbles the driver as he snaps his whip.

The horses strain in their harnesses and the wheels roll forward. The carriage rattles across the bridge and is gone. After a minute, I don't hear any more barking. Just the chirp of the chickadees. They sound so cheerful and I hate them.

REVENGE

March–May 1812

Father watches me closely from the other end of the table. The smell of fresh air floats through the open window — but not nearly as strong as this other aroma.

"Don't breathe in the fumes."

He's letting me help clean the pistols. Wipe the spirits on the metal, and at first you see all the colours of the rainbow. When you rub them away, the smell remains. It makes my head feel light. Makes me feel as if everything's going to turn out all right. Makes me sleepy too.

Sometimes I lie awake at night, worrying whether Ginger is safe; worrying that Eli might be kicked out of the Canadas; worrying that war might come. I worry that Father might marry someone and we would have to share this house with strangers. I worry what William and Henry might do next, or that Mina might actually marry William. I worry that I may have forgotten something that I need to worry about.

Maybe if I smuggled a bottle of the spirits up to my room and took a little sniff, I would fall asleep. But I'm not supposed to breathe this smell. I'm not supposed to handle the pistols either, except under Father's supervision.

Father reaches across the table and takes the pistol to examine my work.

"You've missed the powder hole."

He passes the pistol back to me. If the hole is blocked up with rust or burnt gunpowder, the pistol won't fire. The enemy will shoot first and you'll be dead.

"Will you teach me how to shoot it?"

"You think you're strong enough?"

"Eli's pa lets him fire pistols, *and* their big Kentucky rifle. *And* he says that if he joins a flank company, he'll fire the Brown Bess musket too." When Father doesn't respond, I add, "He looks old enough."

Father nods. "But I know he's not sixteen, and Magistrate Dunwoody knows he's not sixteen, and General Brock knows he's not sixteen. And that's the end of it."

"He could join in another county — where they don't know him."

He chuckles and wipes oil onto the second pistol. When he is finished, he sets it in the satin lining of a walnut box. The box also contains two ramrods, two pistol balls and a flask so small it would hold powder for only two shots. Each has its place in the red satin.

* * *

"Them's *real* duelling pistols?" Eli asks.

"They're not duelling pistols." I lower my voice. Cathleen is in the kitchen, and there's only the lobby between us. "They're from the war."

He shakes his head. "Sure look like duellers."

"Why would Father own duelling pistols?"

He shrugs. "Your pa ever killed anyone with them? In the war, I mean."

"He almost never talks about the war."

Eli reaches for one.

"We're not supposed to touch."

Eli looks at me with sad, puppy eyes, then grins like an imp. *Just this once.* His eyes widen. "Corn, Slim, this here's heavy."

Eli holds the pistol butt in both hands in front of his chest, pointing the barrel up to the ceiling.

"Take the other one."

I hesitate.

"Go on, Jake." Eli nudges me. "Try it out."

"I've held it. Lots of times."

"Just for me."

I carefully lift the pistol from its place in the satin. I copy Eli: shoulders back, pistol in both hands, pointed up.

"Ten paces."

"Eli!"

"Ten paces and turn."

"The dining room's too small."

"Eight paces, then. Little ones."

He has to circle around the rocking chair to reach the doorway. My route veers around the table to the corner.

"Now turn."

He's so close. How could anyone miss?

"Take aim."

He raises his pistol with both hands. When it's pointed right at you, the barrel of a pistol looks enormous.

I keep my voice steady. "You're not supposed to stand that way."

"Says who?"

"Mr. Willcocks."

"How does he know?"

"He knows lots of things."

Eli's eyes widen. "Has he been in a duel?"

I shrug. "He says you don't stand like that."

"How, then?"

"Sideways. So you make a smaller target."

He nods, then turns with his right shoulder toward me and raises the pistol again with one hand. The black hole wavers before me. "Corn! Jake, it's too heavy. How they ever aim these things?" He lowers the pistol and turns it around, holding it by the barrel. "I'd just as soon use it as a club and hit Junior over the head."

"What?"

"Can't you see it? Junior and me on the field of honour. He aims. He fires. He misses. And I just walk over and club him."

"Eli, these aren't duelling pistols. And you're not going to use them to settle our score with William."

"We gotta do something, Jake. We gotta get them." He ponders a moment. "Set a bear trap maybe."

"Maybe a bear pit. Dig a big hole and put a bear in it. Cover it up so that they step on it and fall in."

"Yeah. Don't need no bear, though. Ginger would do. Just let her at 'em."

I say nothing.

"Sorry, Jake." Eli threads his way back around the chairs. "You'll get her back. I know you will."

As Eli makes his way back, he pulls the ramrod from the stock. He taps it into the barrel, as if he were loading. Then he stops and looks at the ramrod more closely.

"You could use this thing too." He strikes a sword-fighter's pose.

"Eli . . . "

"Maybe not a sword. But you could use it in a knife fight, maybe."

He slips the ramrod back into the stock, and returns the pistols to the satin.

"What's them letters?" He points to the brass plaque on the side of the box.

"What? Those initials? I don't know. Just something on the box."

"J. J. W. That someone's name?"

"Can't be. My father's name is Robert Jacob Gibson — R. J. G."

Eli shrugs. "Maybe it's someone else's pistols then. But I think you're wrong about them."

"Eli, you're *not* going to club William with them."

"No, not about that. This box? Fancy red cloth? Tiny powder flask? Two balls?" He looks up at me. "Them's real duelling pistols, Jake."

* * *

I've received my very first letter. It was addressed to me. No one else was allowed to open it — not even Father. It's in reply to the letter I wrote to Mr. Willcocks and I wait until I am alone in my room before I read it.

My letter was very short, and it seems that Mr. Willcocks can sometimes be brief too. His letter was shorter than I expected, given the way he talks.

York, Upper Canada

Dear Master Jacob:

It was a pleasure to receive your letter. I hope you and your father are both well, and please give my regards to the wonderfully capable Miss Cathleen. Tell her I miss her beef puddings.

Last week, your Ginger accompanied myself and my friends, Mr. Mallory and Mr. Markle, out for a dinner. And such a dinner it was! We feasted on roast beef, omelettes and pancakes, currant tarts and a very tasty custard pudding.

The Assembly's business takes much of our time. General Brock makes a most effective president of our proceedings, even if we disagree on many things. When the Session ends, I will return to Newark. Would it be safe to bring Ginger back, or shall I make further arrangements here at the boarding house?

Your obedient servant,

Joseph James Willcocks, Esq.

I read the letter over again, and then it occurs to me: Mr. Willcocks's initials — J. J. W. Were the pistols his? Were they ever used?

I go back downstairs and find paper and a quill to write another letter.

* * *

The sun climbs higher. The snow melts and the ice on the lake shrinks back. We tap the maple trees for syrup, and the fishing boats venture back onto the water. The fruits and vegetables in the root cellar have dried and shrunk, but now we have delicious toffee and lots of fresh whitefish.

The docker boys come out from their hibernation. All winter it seems they've huddled with their families behind the shuttered windows of the shanties. When it's time to barter for fish, I go to the docks with Eli. He gets along so well with all of them, and I think their mothers might offer us a better price as a result. Maybe not, after a long winter. But he puts a smile on their faces.

Although I've lived here all my life, and everyone in town knows everyone else, he introduces me. "You know my friend Jake? He works for the *Guardian*."

Few of the docker boys can read. None of their fathers can vote. But my association with Mr. Willcocks raises me in their minds.

Some of them ask me what happened to my dog. "She's run away."

The docker boys are very sorry to hear this. Ginger was popular everywhere, it seems — except with William and Henry. It's still not safe for her to return.

I'm desperate for news about her, and finally another letter arrives.

York, Upper Canada

Dear Master Jacob:

Thank you for your letter. I am sorry for the delay of my response. Things have been more than a little busy. General Brock threatens to dissolve the Assembly and call an election. He thinks he can get rid of my friends and myself that way. We shall see!

I can assure you that Ginger continues to prosper. As you suggest, she will remain at the boarding house with Mrs. McGillicuddy. I hope that eventually it will be safe for her to return, but shall leave that decision to you.

You inquired about the walnut box and the pistols. Yes, they are mine and your father has been good enough to hold them in safekeeping. I don't care whether I ever see them again. They were used in the duel that killed a good friend of mine, Bill Weekes. He taught me what I know about politics, and I carry on his fight for the people of Lincoln County.

But I would give up my office and my position in this community if only we could have him back again. I shouldn't have agreed to be his second. I should not have let him use my pistols. I should, instead, have insisted that he come to some kind of a settlement with the man whom he had wronged. That man, by the way, has prospered since Bill's death.

And so if I have any advice to offer you, young Jacob, it is this: Stay close to your friends. Protect them and keep them out of trouble. No matter how difficult that may be at times. In the end, they will thank you.

Yr ob't sv't,

Joseph James Willcocks, Esq.

* * *

Down by the lake, frogs court one another, some in high-pitched chirps, some in deep garrumphs. In the darkness across the water, a loon calls. The lighthouse beam pulses. I've built a little campfire. I'm lonely waiting out here without Ginger.

Another loon call — closer this time. *Whoooo-OOO-oo-oo-oo.*

A pause.

Then an owl — *Hoo-hoo-HOO.*

I raise my chin, then pipe a loon's reply — *WOO-oo-oo-oo-oo.*

Footsteps crunch on the gravel in the darkness below. A moment later, Eli stomps up the embankment. With both hands, he lifts a jug.

"Now you're gonna see just what makes my pa famous in five counties."

"Eli, I'm not so sure about this."

He heaves the jug to the ground and it lands with a *thud.* Then he sits with his knees crossed and lifts it to his lap. "Back home, he used corn. Up here, rye is best." He unplugs the cork and already I can smell the sweet whiff of alcohol. "God bless George Washington." He grins, then he lifts the jug to his lips and his Adam's apple bobs twice.

The jug comes back down. Eli stares wide at nothing. "Whooo-ee!" He shouts and shakes his head. Then he lifts his face and howls at the moon. "*Awwooooo!*" The frogs stop chirping. Silence. He holds out the jug. "Your turn."

"Eli, I'm not so sure . . . "

"We gotta do these things. Together. We're blood brothers."

I lift the jug. The smell is much stronger than the brandy they gave me when I fell through the ice.

"Eli, I can't. I'm sorry."

I wonder if I have insulted him, but he shrugs and reaches across for the jug and takes another swig.

"So . . . you bring your pa's spirits?"

I reach into my coat pocket and pass him the glass bottle. He removes the cork and sniffs and his eyes go wide.

"It's not for drinking," I warn. "And Father says you shouldn't even smell the fumes." He gives me that mischievous grin. "It's for cleaning things, Eli."

His face gets serious. "It burns real good, I reckon. You ever try it?"

"It's too expensive."

He tips the rim, pours a little pool into his palm and stretches his hand over the fire.

"Don't waste it, Eli . . . Gosh!"

My little campfire flares up and the flame leaps for Eli's hand. For a moment, his palm is aflame, and he waves it fast and tucks it below his armpit.

"Whooo! That's great!"

I snatch the spirits back. He takes another drink from the jug and sighs like a contented piglet. We settle back down to the ground across the fire from each other.

I look deep into the flames. They dance high in colours. When the spirits have all been consumed, I rise and fetch more sticks and put them on the fire.

Eli just sits there with his chin in his hands, watching the fire. But he no longer smiles. His mouth is turned down and his brow so low.

"What's the matter?"

He stares at the flames so hard, it might be the glare of his eyes that combusts the wood.

"Eli?"

His legs are crossed, his elbows on his knees, his chin in his hands, and he does not move.

"Eli?"

His stare withdraws from some point deep in the flames. He straightens his shoulders and rests his hands on his knees. Finally he looks across at me.

"Slim, it's time you and me got those two."

"I just want my dog back." I sit down again on the other side of the jug.

"We gotta hit 'em. Hit 'em hard!"

He lifts the jug. "Eli, that's not a good idea . . . "

He passes it to me. I put it down in the grass.

"Bear pits," I suggest.

"No more daydreams, Slim. For real." He reaches

for the jug. "As you say, we ain't gonna challenge 'em to a duel."

I watch him closely, listen to the inflection in his voice. He's joking about the duel. That's a good sign.

At least, I think he's joking.

"They probably shoot better than we do," I reply.

Eli considers this. "They burned down Pa's shed," he says slowly. "Maybe we should burn down their house."

I laugh softly. "Can't burn down a brick house. Not from the outside."

"Yeah. I reckon. Not even with your pa's spirits . . . But the stable's wood."

I reach over and grab the jug and put it out of his reach. "You don't want to hurt the horses."

He stares out into the darkness.

I offer, "The outhouse maybe?"

He chuckles. Wherever some devil took him deep into the flames, he's now back.

He says, "We'd catch Junior with his trousers down to his ankles, and his butt in the hole." He reaches for the jug but he's unsteady and he topples over onto his elbow and giggles.

I reply, "He probably uses the chamber pot."

"Yeah." He needs both arms to push himself upright, then to rise to his feet. "That Mrs. Hawkins cleans it out for him. Wipes his bum too, I reckon."

"Eli, that's disgusting."

"C'mon, Slim." Eli reaches out to help me to my feet.

"Where?"

He can't quite keep his balance and we both nearly fall over. He rights himself and starts to walk away.

"Eli . . . "

He stops in a wide stance, then turns to look at me. "The campfire."

He makes his way back, taking special care to walk a straight line. He unbuttons his trousers and a stream of pee douses the flame in a hiss of steam.

"Let's take the wood," he says.

He squats down and reaches for a stick but pulls his fingers back sharply. "Too hot," he mutters. He puts his scorched fingers into his mouth while he considers. "Let's go."

He turns once more toward the town.

"Where?" I ask as I try to catch up.

The moon gleams on the rooftops of the houses. Eli heads down the road and cuts up toward the orchard. I realize where he's heading.

"Eli, stop . . . "

"It's your idea — the outhouse."

"Eli, I was *joking.*"

He stops and faces me.

"*I* ain't. We gotta hit 'em back. No bear traps. No bears. No duelling pistols. This is real."

"You'll go to jail. They'll send you to Botany Bay. They could even hang you."

"Naw. They wouldn't do that." Then he looks at me. "Maybe if we burned down the house, they would. But they ain't hanged Junior or Lug."

"This is different, Eli."

"Danged right."

He pivots and heads across the orchard, wobbling a little through the grass. He doesn't stop until he reaches the fence behind the Dunwoody stable.

"What if someone gets hurt? What if it spreads to the stable?"

"I'll be careful. Just give me the spirits."

"Eli, think about this."

"You do the thinking, Slim. You're good at that. It's time to act. And that's *my* job." In the moonlight, his face is hard and resolute. Then it softens as he looks at me. "Slim," he says in a quiet voice, "you're the best blood brother I could ever have."

Something about that expression in those eyes — almost a longing, a goodbye. I've seen that before. Where?

He hoists himself over the fence and stumbles onto the other side.

I must stop him. I can think of only one thing to do.

When I come down on the other side of the fence, I pull the bottle out of my pocket.

I hesitate a moment. Then douse the left sleeve of my jacket.

Eli's having trouble rising to his feet and I stand

over him for a moment. I grab him from behind with my right arm.

"Hey!"

My left arm wraps around his face and I squeeze with all my might. He twists his head, and his left arm is free so he jabs it into my gut. I hold on.

"What the . . . Jake! Get offa me!"

The words are muffled beneath the sleeve of my jacket. I hold like I was catching a chicken.

"Jake!" The word is softer now, and his shoulders are losing their strength. "You weasel . . . "

His muscles go soft and he flops to the grass like a puppet whose strings have been cut.

I prop up Eli's head and rest it on my lap and study his face to make sure he's all right. He breathes. Slowly. Steadily. In deep sleep. Whatever dreams he may have are not peaceful. The frown on his brow won't relax.

What do I do now?

I pull my legs out from under his head and take his jacket by the shoulders and heave him toward the fence. He's as heavy as a sack of corn. I pull once more but drag him only inches. I might get him to the fence, eventually, but never over the rails. I scramble back across the fence and run as fast as I can down the road toward the lakeshore.

At the back of the McCabe house, I tap very softly on the window.

A girl's voice hushes from the darkness inside. "Not tonight. Ma's up with the baby."

I tap again. Mina's face appears at the window.

"Jake?"

"It's about Eli . . . "

She looks back into the darkness, then disappears.

I wait across the road, not knowing whether she'll appear. A door squeaks and in a moment she's beside me, a shawl wrapped around her shoulders.

"He's up the road. At Dunwoodys'. Knocked out. I did it."

"You?" She tilts her head and gives me a look up and down.

"I used Father's spirits. Eli's out cold."

"What you two doing up there?"

"Mina, he wanted to burn down the Dunwoodys' outhouse."

"My little brother?"

We stride up the road in the darkness.

"I don't know what's come over him, Mina. He's going to get himself hanged."

She looks at me hard. She opens her mouth to say something, then thinks better of it. We walk on.

"What is it?" I ask.

"Nothing."

"What *is* it?"

"He didn't tell you nothing?"

"He wants to get back at William."

She won't meet my eyes.

"Mina, is there something I should know?"

"Nothing 'bout our family's plans?"

"What is it!"

"He'll tell you. It ain't my place. Now, where's that little brother of mine?"

We find Eli fast asleep in the grass. We each take a shoulder and, together, we pull him over the fence and drag him across to the orchard.

"You got smelling salts?"

"At the store."

"Best fetch 'em."

I run back in the darkness. Down the road, the rooster crows.

Father's window is open and I hear him snoring as I sneak through the door. He sleeps soundly. Good thing. It used to be Mother who woke up at every stir and noise in the night. She used to poke her head into my room, and I'd pretend to be asleep. She looked at me with . . .

Those eyes. Eli's eyes when he said I was the best blood brother. Mother's eyes as she lay on the bed with baby Charlotte beside her. Sad. Longing. Loving. She was saying goodbye.

I run back to the fence even faster. Eli lies sleeping with his head in his sister's lap.

"Mina, what's this all about?"

She takes the smelling salts without looking at me.

"Mina . . . "

She won't look up as she uncorks the bottle. "He'll tell you in his time."

She passes the open bottle below Eli's nose. His head jerks. His eyelids flicker. He mumbles something and we lift him to his feet.

"Mina, what's got into him? What's happening?"

But she says nothing until we reach the McCabe house. The sky has grown light grey.

"You best stay here, Jakie. I'll do the explaining to Ma."

"What will you tell your mother?"

She giggles. "Reckon maybe you two was out for a toot with a bottle of Pa's brew. That'll explain everything."

Maybe. But there's a whole lot more explaining to be done. What has Eli not told me yet? And how do I explain why I turned on him?

END OF THE BROTHERHOOD

May 1812

Monday morning. Usually Eli walks to the school with me, and this morning, there's so much we have to say to each other. The clock ticks in the dining room and I wait in the lobby, my books strapped together by the door. I wait some more. Then I've waited too long and grab the books and dash outside.

Which direction? The road to the right leads to the schoolhouse, but instead I run through the back garden and past the stables toward the lake. I see him trudging along the beach with a fishing pole. He uses it to slash at driftwood.

"Eli!"

He doesn't turn around.

"Eli!" Stones crunch beneath my feet.

I reach out for his arm and he spins around. I stop cold. He's never looked at me like this before: mouth taut as a fishing line.

"You bushwhacked me."

"Eli, I was trying to protect you."

He scoffs. "I don't trust you no more, you *traitor*."
He spits out the last word and it stings like lye.

"If you let me explain — "

"Don't matter to me none. We're pulling heel."

"What?"

"Pulling heel. We're moving back south."

"*What?*" This must be the news that Mina would
not tell me. "When?"

"Soon as Pa sells the tannery. We're through with
this town. Through with the magistrates. Through
with the bullies. And now I'm through with *you*."

"You . . . you didn't tell me."

"I was gonna. After we got back at Junior." From
across the town, the school bell rings. Eli looks past
my shoulder in that direction and sneers. His eyes
meet mine again. "You best go join the rest of 'em."

"We're blood brothers."

"Not no more."

He spits on his hand, the one he cut to make our
blood oath. He wipes it on his trousers.

"You can't just end it, Eli!"

He looks past me up the shoreline. "You go back to
Old Buzzardnose. Stick with your own kind."

He turns and stalks away. I don't move. Just watch
him grow smaller down the shoreline. It's as if I've
forgotten how to walk.

* * *

A dozen pairs of eyes stare at me from the desks as I tiptoe in. But not the Reverend Mr. Burns. The dominie has his back to the class as his chalk squeaks on the blackboard. I sneak to my desk.

"Master Gibson!"

"Yes, sir!"

He turns so quickly that his black gown swirls.

"You have decided to grace us with your presence."

"I'm sorry, Master." I glance quickly to where William and Henry smirk at me, oversized in their small chairs.

"Eyes front, Master Gibson."

"Yes, sir."

He reaches to his desk and picks up the hickory switch. He holds it behind his back and *tap tap taps* it against his shoulder blades. "Will you take your punishment now or after school?"

"Now, sir."

"Step forward."

Dominie Burns is well practised in the teacher's art of hitting only the fleshy part of the palm. I won't blink. I won't cry out. I stare at the words on the blackboard and somewhere there's a sound of hickory thwacking on flesh. I won't rub my hands.

"Take your seat."

"Yes, Master."

I return to the desk with my palms on fire. I use the pain to take my mind off the heaviness in my heart.

Eli is leaving! If I could restore his trust, I would take this punishment every day. But I did the right thing that night. I know it, even if he doesn't.

"Class," announces the dominie, but I'm not listening.

Then he's saying something about the election, so I suppose I should. Something about General Brock dissolving the Assembly because of . . .

" . . . troublemakers and rabble-rousers . . . " The dominie may be talking about Mr. Willcocks. He raises his voice. "Master Ecker."

"Yes, sir." Henry uncurls himself from his seat and rises.

"I believe you have some news. Would you care to share it with us?"

"Thank you, sir." Henry turns to the class. "It's about my older brother — Abraham. He is running to be our representative in the Assembly."

This is news to me. I wonder if Father has heard.

"On what platform will he be running, Mr. Ecker?"

"Loyalty and duty, sir. Support General Brock and the King."

"Thank you. Be seated." The dominie sweeps his eyes across the room and rests them on me. This time I cannot hold them and I look away.

"Master Ecker is right. We need representatives who will back up the General in these troubled times — not fight him for their own crass purposes. I know you all join me" — he stares at me — "in wishing Master Ecker's brother every success."

* * *

At lunch break, the other scholars scramble into the sunlight. William and Henry stand at either side of the doorway. William studies an apple in his hand, then bites. I can hear the juicy crunch.

When I try to pass between them, Henry puts out his hand.

"Too bad about your friend," says William.

Have they heard that the McCabes are leaving? Did they know even before I did? But I try to keep my surprise off my face, and I mutter, "There's nothing wrong with Eli."

Henry's big arm stiffens to block me. "Not the Turd Boy. I mean Willcocks. He's going to lose this election."

On the other side of the door, William shrugs without taking his eyes from the apple. At this time of year, the orchards are full of apple blossoms. The apples in our root cellar have lain there for months and are shrivelled and dry. But this is a wonderful apple, so big and juicy. Where did it come from?

"Don't be in such a hurry, Jacob." *Jacob?* I can't recall William ever calling me by my first name. He takes another bite of the apple. "Henry's brother will win, no doubt. But in the meantime, we should all get along." He holds the apple easily in his long fingers, and his other hand reaches out to rest on my shoulder. "Don't you agree?"

I shrug his hand away. "You want to kill my dog."

"Your *dog*? I'd forgotten about him."

"Ginger's a girl."

"Quite." And he smiles at me with his straight, white teeth. "But I don't suppose Henry has quite forgotten. Have you, Henry?"

"I *could* forget about it," Henry says. "Friends should let bygones be bygones."

I say nothing.

William laughs. "I don't think we've treated you with the proper respect. Your father was a hero."

"My dog is a hero too."

I push past them but William reaches into his coat pocket and holds out another apple — as big and fresh as the one he has bitten. Where could he possibly have gotten fresh apples at this time of year?

"Gibson, you're smart. We just want to swap some ideas."

I can't take my eyes off that apple. The skin is so firm and shiny. "I'm for Mr. Willcocks. So is my father."

"That's fine," says Henry. "We'd rather talk to someone who's passionate about the election." I reach for the apple. I bite and feel the juice squirt inside my mouth and smell the wonderful aroma of fresh fruit.

With my mouth full, I say, "You'd put people in jail without trial."

"Only dangerous people."

"And who decides who's dangerous?"

"General Brock would have the final say. He's a great man, the General."

I gesture with the apple. "He's a fine general. But he's the general *and* he's the head of the government. Now you want to put him in charge of the *law*?"

"There! You see?" smiles William. "It's very enjoyable to discuss these things with someone intelligent. Come and talk to us, Jacob. Your friend Willcocks — we'd be interested to learn what he makes of all this."

Ah, so that's what they're about. They want to pump me for information about the election.

"You already know what Mr. Willcocks thinks," I shoot back. "Read his newspaper."

But Henry still thinks he can worm information out of me. "What's he really like? Do you think he'll spend much time campaigning?"

They must think I'm pretty naive. "You want me to *spy* on Mr. Willcocks."

William studies me with his catlike eyes before he replies. "We just enjoy the conversation of someone who shares our love for politics."

"Yes," Henry interrupts, "and my brother would like to talk with you too."

William smiles. "Henry's brother will be able to do things for his friends if he's elected."

"Once he's elected," Henry corrects. Then he asks, "That dog of yours, did it ever show up?"

"No."

"She meant a lot to you," William says.

"*You're* the ones who told Mr. McKenney to shoot her." I bite down angrily on the apple. It no longer tastes the same.

"We could change that, you know," Henry says. He folds his arms and leans back against the door frame. "We can do a lot for our friends."

I turn and walk away. I spit the apple out and toss the core over my shoulder.

Henry calls to me from the doorway. "Think about it. Dogs, politics, anything. Talk to us."

I keep walking.

* * *

The days grow longer, but just when I think summer is on its way, a cold wind whips across the lake. I shiver in the growing dusk. The smoke from the McCabe chimney flees to the south, but a light in the windows shines warm.

Over the pounding of the waves, I hear laughter in the McCabe home. That's little Benjamin, squealing with excitement, and there's Jed yelping, "No, Pa! No!" And there's Mr. McCabe's deep voice roaring like a bear. Then that unforgettable sound from my own childhood: someone's blowing on a child's tummy.

"Don't you get them wound up so, Cornelius," scolds Mrs. McCabe, but there's mirth in her voice too.

I sit in the gathering dark where the path cuts through the undergrowth. Not even Ginger to keep me company while I wait and listen.

The laughter rises. "Do it again, Pa!"

Still no sound of Eli. No glimpse of him through the window. No light in the millhouse.

Pulling heel. Eli and his family will pack up everything they own into a big covered wagon, and head down the road. They pulled heel someplace else to come here. Once they arrived, they never even got around to selling the wagon.

But if Abraham Ecker wins the election, and we get martial law, maybe it's best for them to move. And soon!

I give the secret signal. Will he hear it now? Will he even respond?

I cup my hands around my mouth and warble like a loon. A pause. Then three owl hoots.

The door remains closed.

I wait for the laughter to die, and I send the signal again.

If Eli hears me, he ignores it.

He can't just end a sacred oath with spit on his

hand. I've a piece of my mind to tell him, and he'd better learn something about protecting people who matter.

But maybe I don't matter after all.

Behind me, I hear footsteps coming down the path. Too late to hide . . .

I casually walk up the path, as if I'm just out for an evening stroll. A shriek, like a startled animal caught in a trap.

"Sakes, Jacob!" Then Mina lowers her voice. "You sure make a habit of scaring a girl."

"Sorry . . . " There's enough light for me to see the tilt of her head while she studies me.

"You 'n' my little brother made peace yet?"

"What's he told you?"

"He don't say nothing. Just sits around and mopes."

"I was protecting him."

"Yeah, I reckon. But he just don't see it that way. Not yet, anyways."

"He says we're not friends anymore."

She doesn't reply for a moment, then nods her head down toward the lake. I follow her toward the lighthouse.

"Thing about my little brother . . . " She raises her voice above the pound and hiss of the waves. "He's pretty shaken up about leaving."

"He should have told me sooner." I study the pebbles at my feet.

"He don't feel he can trust nobody. Not even you, Jake. Not no more."

"If I hadn't stopped him, he was going to get into real trouble."

"Maybe he reckoned jail was one way to stay here."

Is she joking? "He might get his wish, Mina. If there's a war, they might start putting Americans in jail. You won't even get a trial."

"Yeah." She shakes her head. "Pa'd just as soon pull heel before any of that happens."

"We can fight it, Mina. We can make sure Mr. Willcocks is elected. Then you won't have to go. Maybe. I guess." I pause for a bit. I wish it was simple, but it's not. "I don't know, Mina. You have a better chance if they elect Mr. Willcocks again."

"Truth be told, Jake, I ain't going."

"What?"

"I got myself a job. I'm what you call a domestic help."

"What! Who for? For whom?"

"Let's just say I'm going to be taking care of one of them fine families."

"You're going to work for the Dunwoodys?"

"It ain't official yet."

"But they're the ones . . . Does your family . . . ?"

"Don't tell *no one*. I gotta handle this right." She reaches out, puts her hand on my shoulder and leads me a few steps toward the house. "But the sooner Pa pulls heel, the better for him. Me too, maybe."

I watch her return to the house, then follow. By the time I reach the house, night has fallen.

After she goes inside, I wait on the beach, but the front door doesn't open again. Behind the cabin, I follow the path to the outhouse. If I wait long enough, Eli will have to use it. I hide in the brush nearby. Sooner or later, I'll confront him. But I wait for what seems like forever in this cold wind.

Mr. McCabe is the first to come out and head up the path toward me. The door swings on a squeaky spring. It slams hard against the door frame. There's lots of other sounds too, but I try to ignore those, just like I ignore the smell. I wonder if tanners notice it?

Little Jed makes two trips, and still no sign of Eli. I'm getting so cold and I wish I'd worn an extra sweater. I wasn't counting on waiting around this long.

Then a light jabs across the ground as the kitchen door opens, and I spot Eli's silhouette. I won't confront him when he has business to attend to.

The door slams shut and I wait a minute. Then I give our secret call: the loon and the owl.

"Jake?"

The sharpness of his voice freezes me.

"Jake Gibson? You sneaking about out there?"

The spring squeaks loud and the door slams hard. He's buttoning up his trousers.

"Where are you, you weasel?"

I step into the pathway. "Eli, we have to talk."

"Got nothing to say to you."

"Listen to me."

"Get out of my way."

"We have to stick together, Eli. Now more than ever."

"Now?"

"They're going to impose martial law. They'll put your pa in jail."

"He ain't done nothing wrong. He swore their oath."

"They want to change the rules."

"Ain't that just like them . . . "

"Junior and Lug — they want me to help them. If I do, they say they can save Ginger."

His fists are on his hips and his coat is unbuttoned. He leans forward and juts out his chin. "Well, ain't that just fine."

"But they want me to spy on Mr. Willcocks."

"And you'd do it too. You ain't got no loyalty, Jacob Gibson. Can't trust you for a minute."

"You take that back."

"Truth hurt?"

"I saved your neck."

"You *betrayed* me."

"I stood by you."

"Just like your pa betrayed his country."

"What?"

"You heard me. You're all a bunch of traitors."

"You take that back!"

"Your pa fought for them Tories."

"Take it *back!*"

"Traitor . . . "

And I swing at him — that out-thrust jaw. He's quick and dodges back, but I rush at him and my left hook hits his ribs. He staggers.

"Take it back!"

I'm punching at him wildly now, right, left, right, left, and he backs away from me, his fists up, trying to stop my blows. I hook high, low, low, high, and he doesn't know whether I'm coming at his head or his ribs.

Then his fist jabs out and catches me square in the eye.

Now I'm the one who reels. I keep my feet, but he just keeps coming on, hitting me hard, hard, hard.

I swing at him again and punch him in the jaw. He says one of those words his pa uses and comes back madder than ever.

I try to block his fists, but I'm backing away, backing away. My feet find the pebbles of the beach. I charge him like a bull and my head smashes into his gut. But he stays on his feet. Twists free. Brings his right in an uppercut and catches me under the jaw. I try to find my legs. They're back there somewhere. I just have to keep hurtling back to stay on balance.

My feet splash into the water. The shock of the cold jolts me upright. I step forward to go at him again.

But he's ready.

His left comes at me.

My head rings and the world spins. And the world is very cold. And wet.

I'm sitting in cold water, my arms holding me up in the lake. A wave crashes over my back and slaps me in the face.

He stands over me, his fists ready in case I come up swinging. Then he lowers his guard and stretches out a hand to help me up.

I use one of those words of his pa's.

He stares at me a moment, then sloshes his way back to the shoreline.

He turns at the water's edge. "You go ahead. You talk to Junior and Lug. You're one of them now." He stomps up the slope toward the house and shouts, "Always were."

I lift myself up. I look around. Yes, there it is — upstream where the river enters the lake: the spot where Eli saved my life one winter.

Seems so long ago now. A different world. A different Eli. A different me.

POLITICS
May 1812

Now that General Brock has dissolved the Assembly and called for new elections, Mr. Willcocks comes to our house often. He took one look at my black eye and said something about needing to keep me hidden along with Ginger. Father explained what I told him — that I got kicked by Dolley while milking her.

Three of us at the kitchen table study the list of voters. I can see it through my one good eye. The other is swollen shut.

"McCrimmon?" Mr. Willcocks reads.

"Sound," Father replies, and I put a check mark against the name on my copy of the list.

"Williston?"

"He's an Ecker man."

"Figured as much," says Mr. Willcocks, and I enter an X.

There are over two hundred and fifty people who will vote next month, and Mr. Willcocks wants to make sure that each and every one who supports him will turn out on election day.

"McCarthy?"

"Ecker might buy him."

My head jerks.

"What is it, Jacob?"

"What do you mean, *buy* him?"

Mr. Willcocks snorts. "Oh, there will be votes for sale in the coming weeks, young man. At bargain prices, some of them."

"People *sell* their votes?"

"It happens all the time, Jacob." Mr. Willcocks studies his list. "Votes in exchange for gifts."

"Gifts?"

"Sometimes just a drink after the election."

"That's not a bribe," chuckles Father. "That's just your victory celebration."

I pipe up. "But what about Mr. Ecker? What kind of gifts?"

"Oh, he and his friends have many gifts to offer. He'll have the ear of the Governor. And that" — he looks at Father — "makes all the difference."

Father continues, "Jobs. Titles. Land grants."

"There was a time when I could promise those things too."

"You've done the right thing, Joe."

Mr. Willcocks shakes his head. "Want to sit as a magistrate? Just ask Ecker. Want ten thousand acres in Grand River? Just ask Ecker. Have a cousin who you think should be the next postmaster? You get the picture. And as for Joe Willcocks? All I can offer is to speak the truth."

His shoulders slump when he looks back down at the sheet with the names.

"Can they . . . " I hesitate because I don't want to upset him any more. "Can they . . . keep people from getting kicked out of the Canadas?"

"You mean our friends the McCabes? If Ecker wins, I'd start packing."

"They're already packing, Joe," says Father. "Cornelius is selling the tannery."

Mr. Willcocks looks over his reading glasses. "That so? Didn't hear that in York. We'll have to put a notice in the *Guardian*."

I want to return the conversation to what the winner can do for his friends.

"And what about . . . pardons? If Henry's brother wins, can they give pardons to people? And to . . . dogs?"

They laugh. I don't think it's that funny.

"Sorry, Jacob. Well, I suppose he could. With a word to General Brock. As Administrator, he could pardon."

"Could *you* do that?"

"I'm afraid the General is rather angry with me. Ecker? Who knows?" He looks at me closely. "Is Ecker trying to buy *you*, young man?" He winks at Father. "Is there no end to their perfidy?"

They don't think this is serious. William and Henry do.

I want to say something, but there's a knock at the door, loud and insistent, and we all turn to look.

Cathleen has gone home for the evening. It's up to me to go to the lobby and open the door.

Corporal Porter from Government House stands tall above me. "Is your father at home?" he asks.

I nod.

"Is Joe Willcocks with him?"

What to say? Could Corporal Porter be spying for Henry's brother as well?

"What's the matter, boy?" says the corporal.

A loud voice calls from the darkness, "Carry on, Porter. I will take it from here." The corporal stands aside and General Brock steps forward, filling the door frame. Behind him stands his young aide, Lieutenant Colonel Macdonnell.

"Jacob, isn't it?"

I nod. I close my mouth.

"Staying out of the river, I trust, young man." His voice is smooth as honey. Loud honey. "But not, it seems" — he studies my black eye — "staying out of trouble."

"Our cow . . . "

But he steps past me before I can explain further.

He's already down the hall before I can invite him in.

The kitchen door swings open and Father emerges. "General Brock . . . " His voice trails away. "Welcome." He bows. "Please, come in."

Behind Father, Mr. Willcocks studies the General suspiciously.

"Good evening, General." He bows.

"Willcocks." The General nods. His boots clomp on the pine boards and it's he who leads us toward the parlour. "Glad I've found the two of you together. There's something I want to discuss." I try to follow, but the corporal closes the door and stands in front.

"Perhaps we should be getting some tea for the General," he says. He shepherds me into the kitchen and I put the kettle on the fire.

"Why has he come?" I ask.

The corporal looks at me, one eyebrow raised. "The General keeps his own counsel. And I suggest we do the same."

The most important man in Upper Canada is sitting in our house. If I could, I would stretch my ears all the way to the door, and out past the lobby, and listen to what's being said. How can I get in there?

The kettle whistles. "Would you like tea as well, Corporal?" He shakes his head and fetches the silver tray from the plate rail. I lay out the teapot, cups, saucers and spoons on the tray — just like Cathleen would do. I prepare to carry it to the parlour.

"I'll take care of that, lad," says the corporal.

"I don't mind."

His voice hardens. "The General doesn't like to be disturbed."

"Wait. We need milk." I have a plan. I fetch the creamer. It's empty. "Let me fill it," I tell him, and he waits with the tray in his hand.

I pour from the big milk pitcher. More. Still more. And again more.

"That's enough. Stop. Stop!"

I have filled the china to the very brim. If the corporal moves too quickly, he will spill it over the tray. He stands frozen for the moment I need.

"Here, let me get the door."

"Come back here," he calls, but I'm already through to the lobby. I knock on the door, open it and step inside.

General Brock relaxes his big frame on the settee, while Father and Mr. Willcocks lean forward in their chairs. The lieutenant colonel stands by the hearth. The conversation is too intense for anyone to notice me. And Corporal Porter knows better than to make a fuss. He gingerly puts the tea tray down on the side table and glowers. But his job now is to pour.

"They are not British subjects, sir," Father tells the General. "They are a nation. You must negotiate."

General Brock nods. "I understand, Gibson. Quite." His voice fills the room. "And that is why I need you. And Willcocks."

I slip past the lieutenant colonel to the far end of the room. Seen but not heard: that's the strategy now.

"Assuming that I win the election?" Mr. Willcocks brightens.

"Win or lose," the General replies. "Let's not . . . what do they say here? Let's not beat around the bush. Willcocks, you've been a thorn in my side since the beginning. I called this election so that a new Assembly will help me prepare for war." The General pauses while this sinks in. "But I will say this for you, Willcocks: people listen to you. Including the Grand River Iroquois. I would suggest, sir, that this mission is much more important than whether or not you are elected." He turns to Father. "Gibson, I hope you will accompany him."

"The Iroquois won't be rushed," Father adds. "It may take weeks." Then he looks over at me. "I may need to take my son." All of them turn to me now.

"I have no objections," says the General. I glance at Corporal Porter. He's fuming but he slips out of the room and shuts the door behind him.

"But if you don't mind my being so crass, General," begins Mr. Willcocks, "I think it's appropriate to do a little horse-trading. Just what's in it for us if we pull off this singular act of diplomacy?"

The General stiffens and lifts his chin. "I would have thought, Willcocks, that doing your duty to His Majesty would be sufficient reward."

"That may be, General. But then why don't you ask Abraham Ecker?"

"I won't compromise my agenda," he growls. "Don't try asking for anything that I would not grant you in the ordinary course of my responsibilities."

"So . . . You'll not back down on these suspensions of our liberties?"

"That's how you put it, Willcocks," the General says testily. "I call it preparing for war."

The men remain silent a moment. *Seen but not heard.* But I can't keep myself from speaking.

"General," I offer tentatively, "could you possibly do something for me?" All four men look at me.

Father's eyes shoot me a warning. I have no choice but to ignore it. I have just this one chance.

"You remember my dog, sir? Ginger? The one who helped save me when I fell through the ice?"

The General studies me carefully, but Father's eyes are on him. "That dog," I continue. "She's in trouble. She's hiding now. I wonder . . . That is . . . Would it be possible . . . " I'm babbling like an idiot. *Take a deep breath.* "General, can you help?"

The silence stretches. Everyone looks at General Brock and he stares at me as though I'm some kind of peculiar creature.

Then he bursts into a hearty laugh. "Boy, if that's what it takes to win over the Iroquois, I'll pardon every dog, cat and parrot in Upper Canada."

THE ELECTION
June 1812

Way out there, beyond the gulls and the boats, both the lake and the sky curve away. On the distant line of the horizon, sky blue meets lake blue. But they don't touch. Both sky and water move on and on.

I rest my book on my knee and leave Hector and Achilles as I stare across the distance. I lean back against the willow tree. So many boats on this beautiful day. Fishing dories rest at anchor while their crews cast out the nets. Canoes glide along the shoreline, paddling hard against the breeze. The schooners and barques plough across the water, their sails at full billow. The largest come from the east and Kingston. I'm watching for the smaller ones that sail from the north and York.

Watching and waiting, because today is the day. And tonight we'll celebrate.

I know the boat. I know the captain. And I know the passenger he brings. Mr. Willcocks has arranged for everything.

And now I see her, the *Mississauga*, and on that tack she'll make straight for the river mouth — not much time to run across the fields and through the town and get to the wharves to greet her. But I wait a moment. I wave, and some of the sailors wave back to me.

And then I hear.

Such a joyful bark. Does she really recognize me at this distance? Or is it the familiar lighthouse and the trees against the sky?

Another sound. A splash. And now there's no need to sprint to the harbour. I drop my book and strip off my shoes and my clothes and plunge into the water. Ahead of me a small shape in the water paddles toward me.

She barks. Barks again. The sound is muffled by water.

And when we reach each other, we swim in circles before she rests her paws on my shoulders. She licks my face, and then we both turn together, and swim toward the lighthouse.

* * *

In the middle of the bonfire, a barrel of tar makes the flames burn bright and it will illuminate the market square until morning. But burning tar casts an oily smoke downwind toward the Dunwoody house. I'm sure the noise from our fiddles and penny whistles can be heard down there as well. Maybe loud enough to drown out the flutes and violins of their country dance. The big red flag flaps in the breeze so that you can read the words stitched across it in blue ribbon: *WILLCOCKS*.

Mr. Kerrigan rushes out of the tavern doorway with more drink. Mrs. Kerrigan serves platters of beef carved from the ox that has been roasting all day on the spit. And king of it all, Mr. Willcocks moves through the crowd, shaking hands, slapping backs, and making sure everyone has enough to eat and drink.

Ginger and I sit near the fire and watch the fiddlers and the dancers. Her eyes shine and her tongue hangs out as she smiles. I reach out to scratch her between the ears, but she flinches and draws away. It's been like this since she arrived — she won't let me touch her head. She may be overjoyed to see me, but I think she still hasn't forgiven me for sending her to York.

But now her ears twitch and she closes her mouth to sniff the air. She rises to her feet, barks and trots into the crowd.

"Ginger!" I call, and push my way through after her. I stop.

She lies on her back while Eli laughs and scratches her belly. Then he scratches her ears. He looks up, sees me, and his smile fades.

We study each other a long time. He rises slowly to his feet. Neither of us wants to be the first to look away. He nods down at Ginger.

"She came back?"

"Yes."

The music stops. Somewhere they take their places for the next dance.

"You know where she went?"

"Yes."

I'm not going to tell him more than that. I have secrets to keep from him now. The General's secrets.

The music starts again, so merry and light. Somewhere people are happy.

"They're not gonna shoot her?"

"Not anymore."

His eyes narrow. He changes the topic.

"Pegleg McKenney, he's down at the Dunwoody party."

I don't reply.

"More fun over here," he says.

"Is your father coming tonight?"

"I reckon. He's voting Willcocks."

I know already. Mr. McCabe is on our list. But I don't tell Eli this. I don't say anything.

We turn and watch the dancers. We stand side by side, a few feet apart, arms folded. Finally I ask, "Your father still leaving town?" I steal a sideward glance.

"After the vote," he says. "He swore that oath to

the King. He says he's gonna get one vote out of it before we pull heel."

I turn and face him. "You probably want me to apologize, Eli, but I can't. I did what I thought was right."

Silence.

"You'd have gone to jail if you burned that building."

"I know it."

"You called me a traitor. My father too." He tightens his arms across his chest as he studies his boot and scuffs the dirt. "And I'm not on William and Henry's side. I'm helping Mr. Willcocks, and you should be too."

He doesn't respond to any of this. Finally he looks up. "There's a war coming, Slim." He's used his special name for me, but I still don't trust him. "Your family and my family, they're gonna be on different sides of the border now. Probably on different sides of the war." Then he looks at my chest. "You still have that thing?"

I realize I must have been squeezing the medicine bundle. I stuff it back in my shirt.

He folds his arms again. "Just so's you know, I meant you no disrespect. Your pa neither."

He turns and weaves through the crowd. Ginger follows him a few steps.

"Ginger, here girl." She returns and tilts her head as she looks up to me. She stares back after him and reluctantly follows me to the bonfire. The music doesn't seem so lively anymore.

* * *

Voting day dawns without a cloud in the sky — a promise that the heatwave will continue. A wooden stage has been built outside Government House, shaded by a tent awning. It's called a hustings, and they erect it every time there's an election. For weeks, Mr. Willcocks has been talking about "going to the hustings," and here we are.

An oak table stands in the middle of that platform, and on a big chair behind that table sits Mr. Dunwoody. He wears his courtroom robes and hammers a gavel to silence the crowd. Mr. Willcocks stands to his left and Mr. Ecker to his right. Abraham Ecker looks like an older, less-pimply version of Henry.

Father and Mr. Willcocks aren't happy that General Brock appointed Mr. Dunwoody to run the election. The General probably thinks Mr. Dunwoody is as honourable as he is himself, but Mr. Willcocks is not so sure.

Another three blows from the gavel, and Mr. Dunwoody rises to his feet and gives a speech to explain the rules for voting. This seems about as interesting as one of Dominie Burns's lessons.

But beside me, Father's hand shoots up. "A point of clarification."

"Yes, Mr. Gibson?"

"You say that you will close the election if no one steps forward to vote in the course of one hour."

"That's right, Mr. Gibson. I shall deem that the voting has concluded."

"Will the candidates have a say about when you close?"

Mr. Dunwoody takes a breath. "No, sir. It shall be my decision alone."

The crowd stirs.

"Well, that ain't fair," someone calls from the other side of the semicircle. It's Eli's father, so tall above the rest of the crowd. Eli stands beside him.

Mr. Dunwoody looks down haughtily. "As Returning Officer, I decide what is fair." He pauses a moment, then adds, "Here is my rule. If no one steps forward within one hour of the last vote cast, I shall conclude that the polling is finished for the day. Then I shall announce the winner."

"That's not enough time," Father replies. "Not for farmers to come to town."

"That is my decision, and I believe it to be fair."

Mr. Willcocks steps forward. "This is *not* fair, sir, and I wish to register my protest."

"Your objection is noted," Mr. Dunwoody replies without even looking at Mr. Willcocks.

"Let's get on with it!" a man shouts.

I look up at Father. "There aren't very many of

Mr. Willcocks's supporters here yet, are there?"

Father's mouth is a grim line. He knew this would be the challenge: Mr. Willcocks is popular with the farmers, but most of them must drive for miles to vote. Mr. Ecker is popular with the people in the town, and they just have to walk down the street.

Mr. Willcocks threw the party last night to give his supporters another reason to come to Newark a day early. Some did. But not enough.

The crowd shuffles as the men line up.

"State your name, occupation and residence, sir," calls Magistrate Dunwoody.

"Jeremiah Hawkins. Farmer."

Mr. Dunwoody's hired man. He's not a farmer.

Mr. Dunwoody draws a line across the list before him. "You are eligible to vote, Mr. Hawkins."

"One moment, if you please." Father raises his hand. "Mr. Hawkins has no property. Why is he allowed to vote?"

"I believe the roster will indicate that Mr. Hawkins has registered a homestead near Grand River," Mr. Dunwoody replies.

A vein stands out on Mr. Willcocks's forehead. "Since when?"

"Your query has been noted." Mr. Dunwoody turns back to Mr. Hawkins. "Whom do you support?" he calls in a loud voice.

"I vote for Abraham Ecker," Mr. Hawkins declares.

Then he turns to face the crowd. "And I hope you all do too!"

The crowd cheers.

"And you, sir? Name, occupation, residence."

"Cornelius McCabe. Tanner. Newark. And I'm votin' Willcocks."

Some cheer, but not as many.

Mr. Dunwoody frowns at his list.

"We don't seem to have you on the voters' list, Mr. McCabe. I'm afraid you're not eligible."

"What's that mean?"

"You cannot vote, sir."

"I done swore your blasted oath! I own property. A tannery. You can smell it from here. I got the right to vote!"

"We shall inquire as to your eligibility presently. In the meantime, let's proceed."

Mr. Willcocks steps forward again. "Sir, this is a travesty. Mr. McCabe owns property. He has resided here for over a year . . . "

"As I say, Mr. Willcocks, we will look into it."

"What's happening?" I ask Father.

His arms are folded but his hand taps on his lips the way it does when he's deep in thought. His eyes survey the crowd.

He murmurs, "They're fixing the election."

A hand pulls at my sleeve.

"Jake! Jake!" Eli's eyes flit between mine and the

stage. He ignores Ginger's greetings. "Why ain't they letting Pa vote?"

"They're fixing the election."

"They better fix it soon. It's broke real bad."

"No, they're cheating so Mr. Ecker will win."

Eli looks back to the hustings. Each voter steps forward in turn and calls out which candidate he supports, and the crowd cheers. Mr. Willcocks's supporters try to make a lot of noise, but there just aren't as many of them.

Mr. Dunwoody calls out names and I keep the count in my head. Mr. McFarland: Ecker. Mr. Grant: Ecker. Mr. Lawe: Willcocks. Mr. Wiebe: Willcocks. The Reverend Mr. Burns: Ecker. The sun climbs higher.

Ecker: 19. Willcocks: 13.

"Jake . . . "

Ecker: 22. Willcocks: 18.

"Jake, I'm sorry. I should never have called you a traitor."

"Ecker: twenty-three. Willcocks . . . What?"

"Me calling you a traitor. You didn't deserve that. Your pa neither."

I study his face. He looks into mine. His blue eyes don't blink, and neither of us looks away.

"Eli, I'm really sorry I couldn't stop you some other way. I had no right to knock you out."

"Yeah . . . Well . . . Thanks for saving me . . . I guess."

After a moment, he says, "What's the count?"

"I don't know. I'm sure we're losing."

"Guess I shoulda helped more." Then he adds, "Mr. Willcocks could win it yet. Couldn't he?"

I shake my head. "There's no more of our supporters in the line."

"Where's your pa? He ain't voted yet."

It's not hard to find Father. He has moved up to the front of the hustings, but has not taken his place in the lineup. On one side of the porch, Mr. Ecker shakes hands with his supporters. He's already counting on victory. They look so smug.

The last person in line votes. Mr. Dunwoody calls, "Are there any other votes to be cast? Is there anyone who still wishes to vote who has not already done so?" He scans the crowd and his eyes rest on Father.

"Mr. Gibson, sir. Don't you wish to cast your vote?"

Father stands in his place and replies in a clear, calm voice, "I believe, sir, that I have sixty minutes remaining to vote."

Mr. Dunwoody snaps, "This is highly irregular, sir."

"Irregular!" Mr. Willcocks shouts. "What's irregular is your conduct of this whole election! This is a farce, sir! A travesty!"

"Your comments are noted, Mr. Willcocks," says Mr. Dunwoody as he studies his pocket watch.

What's going on? Why isn't Father voting?

"Your pa's pretty smart," says Eli. "Stalling for time like that."

Eli's right: Father has an hour to vote, then Mr. Dunwoody will have to start his countdown again. More time for more Willcocks supporters to arrive.

I scan the faces. "Where is everyone?" Over the past weeks, I have delivered messages to most of them. Mr. Withnall from Queenston. Mr. Wiebe from St. David's. Mr. O'Brien from the farm beyond Fort George.

"Eli," I whisper. "They're all from up the river."

"Who?"

"The men who voted for Mr. Willcocks."

"Yeah."

"There's no one from *down* the lake — beyond Four Mile Creek."

"And where's Junior? And Lug? I reckoned they'd be here, puffed up like pigeons."

"Come with me!"

* * *

Inside the stable, the air is cool, and Solomon huffs in complaint as we lead him into the bright light outdoors. But Ginger wags her tail, ready for adventure.

"Jake?"

"Help me up, Eli." One foot in the stirrup, I heave myself into the saddle.

"Don't you think we need to be prepared?"

I hesitate before swinging my leg across Solomon's back. "For what?"

"No telling what we'll find."

He runs to the house and I slide off Solomon to follow. Cathleen watches us from the shade.

"Where do you two get your energy?" She fans her face.

Eli touches his forehead. "Morning, Miss Cathleen. Can't stay to chat."

He heads straight for the dining room. The air is so close and humid, the sweat soaks my shirt.

"Eli . . ."

He fetches the walnut box from the top of the bookcase.

"Eli, what are you doing?"

He snaps open the hooks.

"What's this?" he asks. Eli holds up a piece of folded paper that lies on top of the pistols.

"That's mine." I snatch it from him. I put it there for safekeeping. I had thought that the walnut box would be the best place to store a precious document. I hadn't counted on Eli . . . "What are you doing?"

He stuffs the pistols into his trousers near the suspender buttons but his face twists in concern.

"Ain't gonna stay like that." He looks at me. "Reckon we need the box too. Let's go!"

"Eli, my father won't let us . . ."

"Come on, Slim. Time's a-wasting."

He tucks the box under his arm. I put the paper down on Father's desk. Then through the window, I see Ginger follow Eli across the yard. I think again. I stuff the paper down my shirt. I just might need it.

THE BATTLE OF FOUR MILE BRIDGE

June 1812

This is how I picture it.

Solomon would carry the two of us as lightly as a saddle blanket. We would gallop down the road, his mane flying in the wind. The miles would disappear beneath the drum rattle of hooves — *gallopa-gallopa-gallopa-gallopa*. Ginger would race to keep up, her tongue hanging merrily and her ears and tail high. On the road, people would stare as we approach. "Hurry!" I would shout as I reined Solomon in and he reared up on his hind legs, his hooves pawing the sky. "Hurry, or the polls will close." They would salute us and hustle toward the town. Meanwhile, we four heroes — two boys, a horse and a dog — would charge deeper into the farm country.

Yes, that's how it should be.

It's not turning out that way.

For one thing, the road to Four Mile Bridge is empty — not a soul to salute us.

For another, I can't work Solomon up to a gallop.

His big hooves canter steadily, *thump-thump-thump* . . . *thump-thump-thump.*

Eli grips my waist so hard with one arm that it's hard to breathe. His other arm clutches the walnut box and its corner digs into my ribs.

The medicine bundle pops out from under my shirt and dangles from my neck. I grab it and stuff it back down my open collar beside the folded paper.

Solomon snorts, then decides he's had enough.

Trot-trot, trot-trot, trot-trot. Eli and I bounce like water drops sizzling on a griddle. He grabs me tighter as he slips over to the side, but I jam my feet in the stirrups. He hangs on and doesn't drop the box.

In the distance, a row of trees. We're near the creek. Ginger gives a cheerful yip and runs ahead.

"Go, Solomon! Go!" Not all the kicking in the world will urge him to canter again. In fact, he decides to slow down even more. His walk feels so smooth after the trot.

"Go!"

"Let him walk, Slim. My insides is so rattled, I think they's outside now."

But I kick Solomon again. He snorts his disdain and plods forward.

Ginger scampers back and barks. Solomon kicks at her, then breaks into a trot again.

"Hang on!"

In the shade of the trees, a dozen horses stand

tethered to a fence. Meshach and Abednego look up lazily and chew grass as they watch us trot by. I smell the creek now, so cool and inviting.

Beyond the trees, the bridge and the buildings shimmer in the heat. On the far side of Four Mile Creek, wagons and carriages stretch back along the road. They cannot cross, and now I see why.

In the middle of the bridge, blocking passage in both directions, a wagon has broken down. It leans at an angle, the rear axle snapped and the back corner dug into the planks. Crates, barrels and sacks have tumbled in a haphazard barricade.

Two men kneel beside a broken wheel, studying it like hunters reading a trail. Two others lift bags out of the way. They move slowly, taking their time. Three others relax against the railing and watch. There's no urgency. Just the opposite: they're stalling.

I've seen those men down by the wharves, loading and unloading the ships that cross the lake. They're the big longshoremen who haul the barrels and crates off the ships. Back in town, they keep to themselves on the docks and in the taverns. They own no property and have no vote in this election. But they're doing a good job for Abraham Ecker's campaign.

That's what they're up to. At the far end of the bridge stand three other people who also have no vote in this election.

There's Mr. McKenney. He takes a wide stance on

his wooden leg and holds a musket across his chest.

Beside him stands Henry with his sleeves rolled up and his arms folded.

In his crisp white shirt and straw hat, William tries to reason with angry people.

I know those people — the ones being stopped from crossing the bridge. Their names are on our list of Willcocks voters.

I kick Solomon harder, but he slows to a walk.

Four steps. Five.

Then Solomon stands in the road, lowers his head and munches on the roadside grass. Ginger braces in a wide stance. She snarls and barks at Henry.

William looks around, then steps past the wagon and over the fallen crates. Mr. McKenney follows as best he can.

"Gibson!" William smiles as he approaches. "Any news from the election? Sorry we can't let you cross the bridge. It's just not safe."

I shout across the creek. "Hurry! They're going to close the polls!"

"You let us through *now*!" someone yells.

Henry calls, "Order, there!"

"Let us get in there," shouts Mr. O'Connell. "We'll have that wagon out of the way in no time."

But Henry shakes his head. One of the longshoremen joins him. He carries a big stick.

William ignores all this. "I see you've brought Turd

Boy." He glances down. Ginger pays him no mind. Her barks bang like pistol shots. "And your dog too," continues William. "It's come back. How happy for you."

Mr. McKenney finally negotiates his wooden leg over the clutter. He stands beside William with sweat pouring down his face.

William doesn't even bother to turn his head to tell him, "I suppose you'll have to shoot the dog after all."

"You leave Ginger alone!" My words squeak.

"I have a warrant for its execution, Gibson," William replies.

Mr. McKenney holds his musket at the ready. His eyes dart nervously between William and Ginger.

William snaps at him, "Well, man, do your duty."

From behind me, a loud *click*.

"I wouldn't be doing nothing rash," says Eli.

Eli's arm stretches past my shoulder. It points a duelling pistol at Mr. McKenney.

Everything seems slower and I notice every detail. Eli's carefully scrubbed hands. The fingernails cut very short. There's a wart at the base of his thumb. The sun is so bright it leaches the colours. The sky is white. The road is pale. So are the faces below me.

It's so quiet. The angry voices at the bridge fall silent. No one slouches on the railing now. Ginger barks. Barks again.

"Bet you it's not loaded," Henry calls from the bridge. Mr. McKenney's eyes flicker with doubt.

"Well, I tell you what, Lug." A second *click*. "Why don't I just raise the stakes?" Now two hands, two pistols poke in front of me. The second one points at William. "What do you think, Junior?" Eli adds softly. "You willing to bet on *that*?"

Eli! What do I do now? Go with it, I guess.

No one else moves, but I swing my leg over Solomon's neck and hop down to the ground. I pull the paper from out of my shirt, unfold it and hand it to William. "This is from General Brock."

"Nonsense!" he scoffs.

"Read for yourself."

He takes the paper and glances down. His eyes skim the page.

Then he looks at me. "How did you ever get this?"

I don't have to tell him. He can see for himself in the General's own writing:

To whomsoever it may concern:

The bearer of this paper, Master Jacob Gibson, of Newark, Upper Canada, has been tasked by me with an assignment in His Majesty's Service.

He is to be rendered any assistance needed, and under no circumstances is any harm to come to his dog, which responds to the name "Ginger."

Ordered by me, this 12th day of May,
Newark, Upper Canada.
Brock, Maj. Gen.

Mr. McKenney peers over his shoulder. "That's the General's signature?" Then he adds hopefully, "I don't shoot the dog?"

"This is outrageous," shouts William. "Why would the General — ? Where are you going? Stop!"

I snatch the paper and stuff it down my shirt as I stride toward the bridge.

"You let those people through, Henry Ecker," I order. My voice cracks. It carries no authority. But now everything moves. It's like I've touched off a barrel of gunpowder.

Ginger surges ahead and leaps over a fallen crate. Mr. McCormack takes a swing at the longshoreman. Mr. O'Connell tackles another man. The farmers rush forward.

Henry fends off Ginger's attack. She bites his trouser leg and won't let go.

A longshoreman runs past me as he bolts down the road toward the horses.

"Gibson! Stop!" William reaches out for my arm but I push him away.

Solomon hurtles past me, his big hooves thumping onto the bridge. Eli bounces up and down. He clutches the saddle with both hands. Where are the pistols? At the barricade, Solomon brakes to a halt and Eli flies forward, right onto Henry's shoulders. They both fall to the planks.

"Gibson, you'll regret — " William grabs me by

the shoulders. I spin around and lunge for him.

Behind me, the thumping and banging of a brawl. Boots on boards. Fists on flesh. Oofs and oaths.

Then a big splash.

No time to look.

I shove at William's chest with every ounce of strength and catch him off balance.

His arms flail. He stumbles against the railing. He leans wildly over the edge and his eyes catch mine.

Those eyes spit venom. Then he seizes control of his face.

His smile pleads.

He reaches out one hand toward me.

But I push him over.

Splash!

I lean against the rail and look down. William sits in the muddy water, his hair plastered to his face, his shirt stuck to his skin. Beside him, Henry rises to his feet, water running off him in rivulets. He leans over to help William to his feet and the two slog their way toward the far bank.

"Jake!"

Eli clings to the railing post, his legs dangling above the water.

Ginger stands beside him, teeth locked in his shirt sleeve as she tries to pull him up.

I push past the farmers as they lift the boxes and sacks from the broken wagon.

I grab Eli under his armpits and heave. He grunts and swings one foot up to the edge. He rolls onto the planks, staring up at the sun, panting.

Behind me, the farmers lift the wagon by the axle and push it to the side of the road. The crowd streams toward Newark.

"Hurry!" I shout. "They're going to close the polls."

Mr. O'Connell snaps his buggy whip and his carriage rattles away. At that pace, he'll reach the hustings in time to vote. Then the clock will be reset once more: another hour for the others to arrive.

Eli stares around at the clutter on the bridge. "Corn, Slim. Never thought you could break a wagon to fix a 'lection."

I sit down beside Eli, catching my breath. "How'd you get Solomon to run?"

"Poked him."

"With what?"

"Ramrod." He nods over to where the pistol's ramrod glints in the sun where it lies in the dust. "He didn't move none when I clubbed his butt with the pistol. But the ramrod did the trick."

Then it strikes me. "Eli, where are the pistols?"

He nods down toward the water. The walnut box lies open, half-floating and half-submerged. It is sinking.

"Quick!"

We pull off our boots.

My toes squish against the mud on the creek bed. Frogs leap away and minnows scurry for shelter.

"You threw the pistols away?"

"Corn, Slim. Solomon was bucking."

The mud sucks at my feet. I grab the box before it slips below the water and toss it back where our boots lie among the weeds.

Ginger splashes in the shallows, pouncing after minnows. Solomon buries his nose in the water to drink.

"Slim, I can't see nothing." Eli wades downstream from the bridge; I'm upstream. "We'll have to feel our way."

His trousers are wet up past his knees, as he gropes the bottom of the stream.

I reach down. Nothing feels firm or solid. But in that ooze and muck, somewhere there's a pistol. Two of them. They can't be that hard to find. Surely they can't. Oh, please, they can't.

I yank at the weeds, but pulling them stirs up the mud and it's even harder to see. I swirl my hands through the black water, stretching and groping. A rotten stick. A waterlogged pine cone. Nothing hard. Nothing permanent.

"You reckon these little fellers will find 'em before we do?" Eli stands with one arm outstretched. With the other hand he tugs at the biggest leech I've ever seen. It has glommed on to his skin. "Dr. Kerr'd pay good money for this one," he says.

I shudder. I don't want to think how many of those things might be attached to my feet, my ankles, my legs. When I reach down, I'm wet up to my crotch and my privates. Now there's a disgusting thought . . .

Just keep looking!

My fingers hit something hard.

"Eli! Over here!" I hold up a pistol in triumph. Water pours from the barrel. I toss it onto the shore.

"How did it get so far from the bridge?" I ask.

"I . . . I . . . I felt the box slipping, I remember that." He wades toward me. "Then I started slipping too. So I had to hang on. Ow!"

His face brightens. He dips down into the water, and raises a pistol by the barrel. If he'd caught the prize muskie at the fishing derby, he couldn't be more proud.

"They'll dry out," he says while we stagger toward the shore. "So'll your magic."

"What?"

He nods at my chest. "Guess we shoulda stripped before we went in."

I look down. The leather of my medicine bundle is soaked to the same dark colour as the pistol box. Tobacco stains run down my white shirt. How stupid of me! It would have been so easy to . . .

The letter!

I pat my shirt, my waist. Nothing . . . Nothing . . . Nothing . . .

Oh my God, what have I done!

There . . . out in the weeds, where the grass meets water lilies. A white rectangle, so sharp against the tangle and clutter of the stream.

"No!" I stumble and fall to my hands and knees. But I stagger up again and splash my way across.

I snatch the paper out of the creek, and it trails a spiral of water, black with ink.

I unfold the sheet of paper, but it comes apart in my hands as easily as dough. The ink runs down the page, and only at the very top can I make out the shape of any words: *To whomsoever* . . .

But even as I watch, those words run, the edges spreading out into the paper until nothing is left but a dark stain.

"Oh no. What am I going to do now?"

I look up at a pitiless sky. The sun has risen to its peak. But not all the power of the midsummer sun will restore the writing to what it was.

"It don't matter, Slim."

Eli's standing across the creek, his hands on his hips. What's he talking about? This is a disaster. Ginger is safe no longer.

"Them words is powerful. Stopped Junior in his tracks."

"But don't you see, Eli? They're gone!"

"Don't matter. They done their job. Ain't no one gonna touch Ginger now they know the General's on her side."

He splashes across to me, puts his wet arm over my shoulder and leads me back to the other shore. "Them pistols? We gotta clean 'em up real good, otherwise they're gonna rust. Even cleaned, they'll rust out sooner or later. But them words? They'll last. Even if they ain't on that paper no more, folks know the General wrote 'em."

We collapse in the grass on the other side. I know Eli's right. Ginger sits beside me and I scratch her between the ears. She licks my face.

GIFT
June 1812

At the Yellow Tavern, the timbers of the bonfire
crackle and blaze, and the sparks rise toward the stars.
The fiddlers reel and the whistles shrill and everyone,
it seems, has something to celebrate. Dominie Burns
has come for a glass of punch. Even Mr. McKenney is
here, sitting beside us on a bench, shaking a paw with
Ginger. She has such a grin on her face, you'd think
it was a dog who won the election.

The music stops. At the table nearest to the bonfire, people start to sing, "*For he's a jolly good fellow.
For he's a jolly good fellow . . .* "

Mr. Willcocks steps up on the table, his face red in
the firelight, and all around us men and women sing
and move toward the fire.

"*For he's a jolly good fellow. And so say all of us!*"

"Friends! Friends," Mr. Willcocks raises his hands
and calls out, but it takes a few moments before the
cheers subside. "Friends," he begins again, "this isn't a
night for another one of my speeches."

I look at Eli. When Mr. Willcocks says it's not time for a speech, it usually means he'll speak for only twenty or thirty minutes — not the usual hour or two.

"I've said most of what I have to say," he continues, "and I'll say it again in the Assembly."

And I'm sure he'll say it again here too. I motion to Eli. The crowd gathers closer, but we slip through toward the edges.

"We'll stand up for our rights as British subjects," declares Mr. Willcocks, "the rule of law and a free press . . . "

The shadows stretch toward the darkness.

"Corn, Slim, even them dockers showed up for a drink."

Yes, it's true. Mr. Ecker arrived before the sun went down to congratulate Mr. Willcocks. Then everyone came to join the party. The only people we have not seen all night: William and Henry. Maybe they're still waiting for their clothes to dry.

"So, why did the General pardon Ginger?"

I have to be careful here. I can't tell Eli everything.

"He wants us to do a job for him. On behalf of King George."

"Really! When do we start?"

I search for an answer that will tell my friend nothing.

"Not for a while. Your folks will have left for the States by then."

His face clouds with sadness. Is it because I've reminded him they're leaving? Or does he realize I'm not telling him everything?

General Brock's mission is secret. Nobody is to know about it. Not even Eli.

Especially not Eli.

I'm to go with Father and Mr. Willcocks to the Iroquois community. It's called the Mohawk Village. Many of Father's boyhood friends live there, including the man who gave me my medicine pouch. General Brock wants the Iroquois to fight with the British if the war should come.

And it looks like it's coming. Any day now.

Eli's face brightens again. "Hey! Maybe Pa will let me stay with you — until the job is done."

In the distance, Mr. Willcocks's voice fills the silence. "And I want to thank my good friend and official agent, Mr. Robert Gibson." The crowd cheers.

"Won't your family need your help?" I ask. "To get set up in your new home, I mean."

"Yeah," he mutters. "I reckon."

The crowd is cheering once again. There's Father up on the table beside Mr. Willcocks, who shakes his hand and presents him to the crowd like he's just won a prizefight — arm in the air in triumph.

Mr. Willcocks calls out, "There are two more people I'd like to thank. Without the help of two young men, I might not be here tonight celebrating

our victory. Many of *you* would not be here either.
You would have been disenfranchised."

"What?" asks Eli.

"It means losing the right to vote."

"Oh."

Then I realize something. "Eli, I think he's talking
about . . . "

"And I want you all," shouts Mr. Willcocks, "to
give a rousing cheer for the boys. Where are they?
Jacob! Eli! Come on up here."

"Here they be," calls Mr. O'Connell, and he and
Mr. McCormack lift me up onto broad shoulders. I'm
there above the crowd while they carry me forward
toward the table. I turn and see that two men have
lifted Eli onto their shoulders too. They carry us in
triumph toward Mr. Willcocks.

It's happening. It seems like a dream. It's my
dream come true. All those upturned faces smiling
and cheering. At us. Jacob Gibson and Eli McCabe.
Heroes.

* * *

Later that night. The sounds of fiddles, fifes and
laughter carry across the fields — a distant murmur.
Downstream, the frogs sing in the bulrushes. The
water moves swiftly in the darkness below our feet.
We hear it gurgle against the pillars of the wharf.

"Up there" — Eli nods behind him, where crickets

chirp in the grass up the slope — "that's where you and me first met. In the snow."

"I remember." I swing my feet above the water. "And down there" — I point beyond the bulrushes — "is where you saved my life."

"Me and Ginger." She lifts her head at the sound of her name.

"And General Brock."

Ginger waits in the silence, then rests her nose on her paws.

"Lotta water passed this here wharf since then."

I look down the river where the moon shines on the lake.

"It just keeps coming. And leaving."

"Where's it go anyways? This water? After the lake, I mean."

"The St. Lawrence River. Then the ocean."

"Reckon you and me could go there sometime? Maybe build us a big canoe."

"You're going the other way, Eli. You and your family. Other side of the river, beyond the Falls."

"Yeah, but I'll be back."

We look into the darkness from where the river flows, and after a while he says, "You ever seen the Falls?"

I nod. Father used to take Mother and me for picnics. In the old days.

"Maybe we could meet there. Your side of the river,

my side, it don't matter. Pa says them Falls is about halfway to where we're going."

"Buffalo?"

"Yeah."

"I like that name — *Buffalo*. It means something." He looks at me. "What's a Newark, anyway?"

"Some place in England, I think."

We consider this a moment.

"Yeah, Buffalo's better," he says. "You ever been?"

I shake my head. "I've never been on your side of the river."

It feels very strange to say this: *your* side, *my* side. It's just a river, but it divides us now in so many ways. I once was willing to cross its ice for him.

"Pa says our new home will be where this river begins."

Eli doesn't have that quite right. I know that the river begins far beyond Buffalo. It starts hundreds of miles farther upstream — many days' travel by canoe. And the lakes up there are even bigger than the one here. No matter how far away, that water will one day pass this wharf. How long would that take?

I think about this, but all I say to Eli is, "I'd like that."

We have so little time left. The McCabes have nearly finished packing the Conestoga wagon. It's full of everything they can possibly carry, and sits outside their home, waiting to be hitched up to the oxen.

There's one thing I want to ask of Eli before they leave, but I don't dare. What if he says no?

I listen to the crickets and the frogs. I take a deep breath.

"Eli?"

"What is it, Slim?"

"Can we be blood brothers again?"

"We ain't never stopped."

"Not even when you were mad at me?"

"That there's a sacred oath, Slim."

"You spat on your hand. You wiped it off."

He bows his head and dangles his feet over the water. "Shouldn't have done that."

"Let's renew the oath."

He looks up at me hopefully.

"I've got your knife. The one you gave me. Right here."

This time, when we grip each other's hand, the drops of blood fall into the darkness of the river.

"The river may divide us."

"The river may divide us."

"The Falls may come between us."

"The Falls may come between us."

"The war may separate us on different sides of the border."

"Huh?"

"There's a war coming, Eli. It will be hard to cross the border. Unless," I reflect, "there's an invasion."

"Okay, all of that. A war may blow everything apart, but it don't matter."

"Eli McCabe is my blood brother and I owe him my ultimate loyalty."

"Jacob Gibson is my blood brother and I owe him . . . What was that again?"

"Ultimate loyalty."

"What does that mean?"

"It means we're not going to fight each other, even if King George and President Madison go to war."

"Sure. I owe him my . . . "

"Ultimate."

"Ultimate."

"Loyalty."

"Loyalty."

For a moment, the frogs have paused. The crickets cease.

"If we spit in the water, how long before it reaches the ocean, you reckon?"

"Let's try."

We lean over and our spit disappears into the darkness.

"Reckon mine reaches the lake first." He looks out across the river to the far shore. "Slim," he says to the distance, "as sure as that spit's gonna get to the lake, I promise you this: I'm coming back here. Coming back to see you."

I stare across the water. "I'll hold you to that." I

pause before I turn to him. "I've got you a present, Eli."

He faces me with a big grin. "Yeah? What?"

I raise my arms and bend my elbows. My fingers find the leather cord at the back of my neck. The slight pressure from the medicine bundle lifts from my chest as I draw it over my head. I lower it around Eli's shoulders and the leather bag hangs across his chest.

"You sure?" he asks, his eyes bright.

"Yeah. I guess it's mine now."

"What?"

"Nothing belongs to you until you can give it away. That's what Father said the day it was given to me."

"I got nothing to give you, Slim."

"You've given me lots."

He tucks the medicine bundle into the neck of his shirt. We both gaze out over the river, waiting for the sun to rise above the American fort.

AUTHOR'S NOTE

This book is a voyage of the imagination that begins in the safe harbour of historical fact. Some characters, like General Brock and Joe Willcocks, are based on real people. In the harbour, I've been piloted by William Kirby, Janet Carnochan, Alan Taylor, Ellwood Jones, Richard Merritt, and many others, including the Niagara Historical Society.

But this book is not a history. Eventually the ship must set sail on turbulent waters of the imagination. If the voyage seems too calm, the storyteller must whip up the seas. The Gibsons, McCabes, Dunwoodys and Eckers are fictional characters. The attempt to smash the printing press was inspired by young men a generation later who wanted to get rid of William Lyon Mackenzie. Upper Canada elections often involved dirty tricks and brawls, which I have added to the challenges Joe Willcocks faced in 1812.

In creating storms, I've been helped by many who have been as important to the imagination as the historians have been to the facts, including: my Ottawa circle, Marsha Skrypuch's kid-crit group, Tim Wynne-Jones and my Banff Sisters, and Pola Nicanna. Special thanks, as well, to Sandy Bogart Johnston at Scholastic Canada and Sally Harding at The Cooke Agency.

What is the destination? If the reader has enjoyed the perilous voyage and the story resonates, then we're safely home at last.